FOOTBALL MANAGER

AGED 12

1st in a series by

B BRIERS

LOOK OUT FOR

TACKLING

RUGBY

2nd in a series by

B BRIERS

For

Nick, Tom, Charlie,

Mum and Dad.

I finally made it into print!

My thanks go to…

The **"FRANKTASTIC!"** design team at Chaos,

Lucy Scott for a FRANKTASTIC narration,

Simon Wood at Dubmaster Studios,

And finally to Emma,

I couldn't have done it without you.

1: THE LETTER

I lie in my room under the cover of darkness (my duvet). The door is barricaded by my army troops. An envelope stamped 'Broadcasting Base' in big red letters lies on my pillow, intercepted as it flew through the letterbox.

"Breathe, Barney. In," sniff. "Out," hiss.

"The Premiership's Football Manager Show has replied," I squeak.

Breathing under control, I flick the letter over on my pillow and analyse it. Thin and light, this is not good news. A good-news letter would be thick and heavy, filled with invitations, details and directions for filming locations.

I peel back the seal.

"Barney, come on, you'll be late for school," Mum calls out from downstairs.

No! No time now! A life-changing letter like this needs time for full concentration. I stick the seal back down and slip the envelope under my pillow.

2: TEAM ISSUES

"Playing in the quarterfinal for your school is an honour," the sports coach repeats five times. Nothing like putting pressure on the team.

None of it's reaching Eddie, the left back, though, who's more interested in dissecting the bogie he's fished from his nose. But Al, our star midfielder and top goal scorer, is listening to every word and nodding about taking an early goal along with Hattie, who plays striker.

Al's hand shoots up. "Shall we try a four, five, one layout today, sir?" he suggests. Al knows a lot about football. He's the youngest of three boys, who are all top players. "Lots of the Premiership teams play it." Rumour on the playground says that Al was offered a Harlimac academy place but he turned it down. Good move, considering their current form.

"Let's just stick to the plan that we're all familiar with," Coach replies. He's not the most adventurous sports coach in the world.

Al's cheeks puff out a sigh. Coach doesn't notice, but I do.

Right now I'd say that Hattie's the most eager player in the team. She's my twin sister. Al's brilliant, but I suspect that he thinks he's better than Coach, which is stupid because Al's only twelve and Coach must've been playing a lot longer because he's really old and he's got a beard. But Coach doesn't know everything. He's got the team line up all wrong in my opinion.

GOALKEEPER

Fergus - Can catch, which is lucky.

DEFENCE

Eddie - Not always switched on to the right game.

Barney (Me) - Solid. Often covers for Eddie's mistakes.

Lizzie - Strong 'booter' of the ball, but barely moves.

Diego – Keen but gets confused and tackles own players.

MIDFIELD

Vijay - Likes to boss other players about.

Al - Best player.

Erica - Puffed out after 20 minutes. Chances on rebound.

Cathy - Tries hard, little legs slow to motor up the pitch.

ATTACK

Hattie - Good all-rounder.

Hugh - Hogs the ball, gets tackled before passing.

SUBS

Angus - Fast runner but not bursting with football skills.

Barry - Always smiling even though he rarely gets to play

Olive - New girl, good skills apparently.

So, unless all the play goes down the right-hand side and as long as there's nothing too heavy after twenty minutes, we might just make it. Otherwise, the goalie has to have a storming game.

Looking down the sidelines I spy Mum, and Grandpa, but where's Dad? He promised to try and get here. Why does he have to play golf today anyway? It's midweek. If he's got the afternoon off work he should come to watch us. Our match is much more important than golf. This is the quarterfinal.

We're ten minutes in, and Hugh flies down the right wing. Hattie's drawing level.

"Cross it, cross it!" I call out, not quite loud enough for them to hear at the other end of the pitch.

Of course he doesn't release the ball, that's why we call him 'Hogger Hugh'. The defender tracks him down but it's too late now, the opportunity's gone. He crosses; the ball deflects off the defender's leg in the opposite direction towards Hattie. The keeper dives right. Al sprints in, chipping the ball over the goalie's head as he scrambles to his feet.

"Goal!" Al, you're a hero.

Pighfield are quick to respond and are straight back at us from the restart. Cathy's chasing down the winger but speed's not her strength. Diego's next in line to stop the attacker. I hope he doesn't try grabbing the guy's shirt again; we don't want to give away another free kick. They nearly scored from it last time. I'm backing up, watching where the central midfielder's heading.

Where's Eddie? He should be level with me. I spot him outside the box on the far left.

"Eddie, over here!" I holler. "Pick up number ten!" He doesn't hear me. I think he's watching the red kite circling in the sky.

Diego is struggling to hold back the attack. I've got two players to defend against. I'm split - my attacker wearing a Harlimac headband or Eddie's number ten – who shall I cover?

"Eddie!" I turn to yell at him. In the one moment that I'm not watching, the ball is passed to my man, and the Harlimac headband chips it left. I lunge at the ball but it shoots by. The attacker's silver boots hurdle over my leg and strike a shot at goal.

Fergus flies into the air and makes a fantastic save, tipping the ball with his fingers out to Eddie, who's still standing outside the box. Eddie clatters the ball up field, out of danger.

"Well cleared, Eddie!" bellows Coach from the sidelines.

3: BIG MISTAKE

My covering for Eddie goes unnoticed in the half-time team talk. In fact, Coach repeats his praise for Eddie's clearance from Pighfield's one shot on target. Perhaps if he'd been defending properly they wouldn't have got a shot at all.

As we walk up the field for the second half, the light rain turns into a power shower. Now I'm glad that Mum insisted I wear a thermal. Al's even got his trademark gloves on. They make him look professional.

"Lucky I tied my hair in a bun today," Lizzie remarks as we stand alone at the back, whilst Al and Hattie make another attempt on goal up the other end of the pitch.

Does she think I care about her hair? "As long as you're not plaiting it," I say without thinking.

Up field, Hattie takes a shot. I hold my breath in hope but the ball flies straight into the keeper's hands. My cheeks blow up and the air hisses out slowly.

"What's wrong with plaits?" Lizzie switches from chatty to snappy. "Don't you like my hair, Barney Frank?" She thrusts her hands onto her hips and looks down on me.

I cross my arms defensively. It's annoying when girls have grown taller than you. I can see all the food stuck in her braces and it makes me automatically scratch around at mine. Behind me I hear Fergus laughing. Twisting my head over my shoulder I smirk and roll my eyes.

"I meant … you know, frizzy hair, in the rain..." I stammer. Sometimes it helps having a twin sister that can talk about hair as if it's alive.

"You might be right. I thought you were being rude but I'll forgive you." She speeds off, which is unusual for Lizzie. "Yours, Barney!" she cries.

Baffled, I watch her race towards an oncoming attacker. He doesn't even have the ball. What's she doing?

Suddenly I see it, the long ball dropping from the sky above me. Automatically, I put my hands up to protect my face, which obviously isn't a good idea when you are standing in the penalty box.

"Barney!"

4: BLAME

Crouching at the edge of the box, I hold my head in my hands. I can't watch. The penalty is my fault, although I think Lizzie could take part of the blame for being annoying. Of course, she was also the one who screeched my name afterwards. If it wasn't for her, the ref might have missed my mistake. It's not like I meant to handle the ball.

Pighfield's centre forward paces back from the penalty spot. He kisses two fingers, taps them on his headband and jogs on the spot.

Fergus, our goalie, fakes jelly legs and waves his hands about.

Headband runs up and fires the ball right. Fergus dives, his octopus arms sucking the ball into his belly.

Fergus, you are my saviour.

***

"Playing in a semi-final for your school is an honour …"

I'm exhausted. I spent so much time covering for Eddie this afternoon, it's difficult to stay tuned in.

"We very lost nearly lost that tie." The coach glares at me before spinning his stare across the rest of the team. It's hardly inspiring.

14

"Missed chances, missed tackles, crucial ones." His eyes roll round to me again. "You need to think about that before the semis."

I bow my head and watch the changing room from under my eyebrows. Al flinches as he holds an ice pack on his bruised ankle. That was bad luck, twisting it in the only rabbit hole on the pitch. He glances over at me.

Hang on; *everyone's* looking at me. Except for Eddie, he's found something far more interesting between his toes.

Two large trainers march up in front of me and I'm hit by a waft of aftershave. Coughing, I look up to see Coach's 'I'm very disappointed in you' face.

"Barney," he says to me quietly, although I know everyone else is listening. "You missed a crucial tackle and caused a penalty today. I'm going to have to think long and hard about your position in the team."

I wasn't expecting that. I was covering for other people! And anyway, I think the way he sets up the team is all wrong, but I can't even croak a reply. On that bombshell, he spins on his heels and leaves, ordering the girls back to their own dressing room.

I swallow and try to concentrate on getting dressed as quickly as I can. I just want to get out and away from everyone.

Nothing like celebrating our path to the semis.

"Don't worry about it," says Al from across the changing room. "Coach is probably in a bad mood because he hasn't heard from that football manager show." The other boys laugh.

"Really?" I ask.

"Apparently, according to my brother." Al's brother is a sixth former and football captain of the first team: in other words, a very reliable source. "Coach told the first team that he'd entered and was waiting to hear from them."

Hm.

"Yeah, Barney, we can't all be heroes all the time," says Eddie as he pulls his trousers over his muddy legs. Has he *ever* been a hero? "I'm glad I did that clearance today to get us out of trouble."

"It was good," Vijay says.

"Yeah, well done," chorus Fergus and Hugh.

Can nobody else see that Eddie is a huge weakness in our defence?

I stuff my dirty kit in my bag then sling it over my shoulder and head for the door.

"See you, Barney," says Al.

"Yeah," I mumble.

"Tell Hattie she was amazing as usual," shouts Hugh.

Those words follow me down the corridor.

At least Dad wasn't there to watch today.

***

Of course, Hattie is quick to fill Dad in on our game as soon as he steps through the front door.

"Sounds like you were lucky to go through," says Dad, carrying his golf clubs down the hall. "I played a storming back nine on the golf course. This beauty," he tells us, picking up one of his clubs and kissing it, "this, gave me a hole in one on the sixteenth. Amazing!"

He opens the cupboard, making room for his clubs. He grins at me. "A hole in one," he says again.

"Amazing," I repeat uninterested. I turn my back and walk off down the corridor.

5: MISSING ENVELOPE

It's been a bad week. I was late to class and had to spend a lunchtime detention doing litter picking in the school playground. Then I was unfairly blamed for a penalty in the cup quarterfinals. I don't think they'll drop me from the school football team. How can they when it's Eddie that's rubbish not me? I'm not hopeful about Harlimac's chances tomorrow either. My football team is fighting to stay in the Premiership.

It can't get any worse.

I pull back the duvet and jump into bed.

'Ah', clean sheets, I sigh lying back under the covers.

"Clean sheets!" I sit bolt upright realising Mum's changed the bed. I flip over to face my pillow, grabbing the Harlimac pillowcase and lifting it into the air. "Where is it?" I panic, staring at the blank space on the mattress. The letter that could change my life forever is gone.

I jump out of bed, pulling the duvet off with me, but there's no sign of the letter. I storm across the room and yank open the bedroom door. I'm about to shout down to Mum and ask where my letter's gone, when I hear another Premiership's Football Manager Show advert blasting out of the telly downstairs.

"Last chance to apply by midnight Saturday!"

I creep to the edge of the landing and crouch down. The lounge door is ajar but all I can see is Dad's smelly feet resting on the footstool.

"Load of rubbish," he moans.

My head drops. I can't ask Mum what's happened to the letter because she doesn't even know I've entered. I'm doomed; I'll never get to show off my sporting talents, ever. I shuffle back into my room, picking my pillow up off the floor and chucking it at the bed head. Bending down, I grab the duvet and tumble onto the mattress, but the duvet gets caught around the bed leg, so it covers only half of my body. I roll off the bed to release the duvet and that's when I spy it.

My knees scrape against the carpet as I scramble to retrieve the letter. It must've fallen under the bed as Mum changed the sheets. I run my fingers over the red stamp, 'Broadcasting Base'. Now in my hands is the envelope that holds my goal. I kiss it once for luck.

Quickly, I tear open the seal and pull out a single sheet of A4. Only this letter knows that the next 'Football Manager' could be me!

Dear Barnaby Frank

Thank you for entering The Premiership's Football Manager Show.

Your entry has been received and logged.

Due to a high volume of entries, we will be contacting you shortly with more details.

Is that it?

6: HARLIMAC FC

Hailstones pelt me as Dad and I run back from the bus stop. When Dad puts his key in the door, Grandpa's still only half way down the street, ambling along under his umbrella.

I peel off my jacket and hang it dripping on the peg in the hallway.

"How was the football?" calls Mum from the kitchen.

"Harlimac lost," I reply.

"Again," moans Dad, "not a single shot on target."

Hattie appears at the doorway into the lounge. She's wearing her Harlimac football shirt over a pair of pink trousers that don't quite reach her ankles. I swear she's grown again, which isn't fair since she's already three centimetres taller than me and we're supposed to be twins.

"We haven't scored in ten games," I mumble.

"Glad I didn't bother coming," she says. "There's a film starting in a minute if you want to watch it with me, Barney."

Grandpa is shaking his umbrella on the doorstep.

Dad walks off towards the kitchen, complaining. "No goals in ten games!"

I can hear Mum consoling him in the kitchen, offering him hot buttered crumpets and a mug of tea.

"Do you want to watch a film with us, Grandpa?" Hattie asks.

He sits on the stairs to untie his laces and remove his shoes. "Is your mum bringing the tea into the lounge?"

Hattie leans back to look through the doorway towards the kitchen. "Yes, come on."

We pile into the lounge to feast on crumpets and muffins and wait for the adverts to finish, when out of the TV blasts...

Have you got what it takes to be the Premiership's next football manager? Transform the fortunes of Harlimac Football Club for an end-of-season charity match. Entry closes this Saturday.

"Ha! Ridiculous." Dad nearly spits out his mouthful of crumpet.

I've got loads of fantastic ideas for training and match play. You don't have to be the world's greatest player to see where Harlimac FC is going wrong. Just having one goal scorer in the team would be a start. And get rid of Agrovio, the striker, he's rubbish.

I scan the room. Mum's not interested in the advert; she's curled up like a cat on the sofa, reading a magazine. Grandpa's taken his tea and retreated to his annex.

"No amateur can help that team, they need a professional," Dad gripes from the wings of his enormous armchair. "The only reason the manager hasn't been sacked yet is because he's retiring at the end of the season."

"Maybe, they need someone different..." I speak up but Dad cuts me off.

"I mean, I was a good footballer in my day," he boasts, delving about in the cushions, searching for the remote control. I want to tell him my secret, but what if he really thinks no one can turn Harlimac around.

"I had the potential to go professional," he continues.

"In the old days…"

"You may mock me, Hattie, but I know about tactics," claims Dad, wiping the crumbs from his mouth with a paper serviette. He nods towards the cabinet in the dining room, where he keeps all his old trophies. He polishes them every fortnight. "Transforming Harlimac FC…." he pauses, shaking his head, "that'll take a miracle."

Oh help, what if they mention my name now? I hold my breath and my eyes pop out. I'm not ready to be announced to the world.

"Didn't I write the details down for you, Barney?" hisses Hattie.

My cheeks burn. I growl like a dog preparing for battle.

But Dad isn't listening. "No one can manage that lazy bunch; it's reality TV gone mad." He finds the remote and aims it at the TV. "Let's get rid of this rubbish."

Coming soon: The Premiership's Football Manager Show – it could be…

The advert is cut short as Dad flicks channels.

"My film!" Hattie squeals.

Dad pulls a face but switches back just as the film begins. He sinks into his armchair, rearranging the cushions and putting his feet up on the footstool.

I slump into the sofa, my face finally cooling. *Could it be me?*

7: PERIPHERAL VISION

I'm alone in the kitchen and spy a batch of Mum's freshly baked cookies on the cooling rack. Time to practice my *peripheral* vision, a skill I've been reading about. If only I'd practised it before the quarterfinals, I might not have given away that penalty. Or if Dad had been there supporting, I wouldn't have made such a big mistake, so it's kind of his fault. Anyway, Grandpa says you learn by your mistakes. Basically, I'm trying to be aware of what's going on around me at all times. Where is the threat of attack? Where are my passing options? I'm like a soldier on the field.

Mmm. I know the cookies are meant for Grandpa's bowls club tea, but they smell so good. Without turning my head, my eyes check right then left: all clear, or so I think.

My fingers reach out for the target.

Wop! A fly swat swipes my hand away.

"Eeeeeeeee!"

"Damn flies," says Grandpa.

I force a grin. Where did he appear from?

"Just come to pick up my cookies," he says merrily. He fills a plastic box with *all* the cookies and walks out of the kitchen. At the door, he stops. "Need to work on that peripheral vision, Barney."

8: THE OPPORTUNITY

Rain, rain and more rain, it hasn't stopped all day. Football practice was cancelled because of the pitch being flooded. We need to practise moves ready for the semis, otherwise we'll never win. After school, Grandpa invites me up to his annex. It's still chucking it down as I climb the steps to his room. I stop to look out the window across the rows of gardens in our road. Soggy, wet, and empty. Raindrops race each other down the windowpane.

How much more miserable can life get?

Sitting in the bay window of Grandpa's annexe is a beige armchair, where I make myself comfortable. A hairy tartan blanket hangs over the back of the chair, tickling my neck.

Grandpa puts a stiff white envelope in my lap. It's marked in big red letters, 'Broadcasting Base'.

Every muscle freezes from my neck to my toes. Even my heart seems to stop.

"Are you going to open it, Barney?" Grandpa is pointing to the envelope. "I assume that this is meant for you and not me." 'Barnaby Frank' is printed across the front in black capitals. It's a reply from The Premiership's Football Manager Show. My heart is now racing.

Without looking up I hand the letter back to Grandpa, otherwise known as Barnaby Frank Senior. We are one of those rare families where Miss Frank, Mum, married Mr Frank, Dad, to become Mrs Frank. So Grandpa, (Mum's dad), has the same surname as me Barnaby Frank. That's why they call me Barney for short.

His lips make an 'O' shape and stay that way as he takes the envelope over to his desk and collects his glasses. I peer at him from under my long fringe. He uses the engraved letter opener I bought him for his birthday to rip open the flap and draws out a single white sheet. I take a deep breath.

With glasses perched on the end of his nose, Grandpa begins to read aloud.

Dear Barnaby Frank,

Following your unusual entry detailing your inventive training methods for the Harlimac Harrier, we are pleased to announce that you have made it through to the first round of The Premiership's Football Manager Show.

I gasp, suck in a fly, and begin to choke. I'm spluttering and gagging. It's disgusting. Grandpa hands me a glass of water and the bin. I hook the fly out, gargle and spit, then gargle and spit again. Yuk! Yuk! Yuk!

"Are you quite finished?" Grandpa asks.

I sit back and grip the arms of the chair, then nod.

He continues reading the letter.

Please respond by email to confirm receipt of this letter. You will then be sent a series of challenges via this email address. In order to secure your place on the show, you must complete these challenges. Your responses are to be judged by a panel of experts. In due course, we will let you know whether you have made it through to the next round.

We look forward to hearing from you.

The Premiership's Football Manager Show.

Grandpa pauses.

My eyes are wide open and so is my mouth.

"*I* didn't enter The Premiership's Football Manager Show," says Grandpa, frowning.

A guilty grin spreads so wide that it threatens to split my face in half. "No, but I did!" I cry. "*Franktastic!*"

I jump around in Grandpa's chair. The back falls away and a footrest pops out beneath my feet. I flop backwards, pinching my arms to check that I'm not dreaming. The blanket falls over my head and the world becomes tartan.

"You just happened to omit the 'Junior' after your name?" Grandpa questions, prodding me in the belly button.

I crease up, giggling. "I forgot!"

"Well you've got one foot in the door, Barney, but you'll need both feet to enter."

Somebody is finally interested in my ideas. My brain's fizzing.

Uh-oh, small problem, I don't have a private email address, only a school one. I can't give them that! Anyway, how will I get to

Broadcasting Base, if I make it that far? This is getting complicated. Help! My mind's a jumble of problems.

"Chance of a lifetime, an opportunity like this." Grandpa taps the arm of his glasses against his teeth.

"Yeah." But the complications blur my thinking channels. My brain's charging through a maze to reach the next round of the show but every route I take is a dead end.

"I'm guessing that they don't know that you are only twelve." He wanders around the room shuffling papers and fiddling with the curtains.

"No." Adults have a way of pointing out the problems that you'd rather not think about.

"You need someone to help you. Someone with their own email address. Maybe a person who shares the same name as you." Sometimes I think Grandpa could be telepathic.

"That would be … Um, yes." I am now trying to send him a message by thinking very hard and staring at the back of his head, sending my thoughts to his brain. I screw up my face with concentration. I hold my hands up to my forehead and point my fingers in his direction.

"I know a thing or two about football." Grandpa turns to face me.

I lean forward dropping my hands down. "Are you saying you'll help?"

His eyes are gleaming. "I wouldn't miss a chance like this for the world."

I leap up and swallow Grandpa in a hug.

"In fact, I've recently devised a little something I'd thought you'd like to see."

He walks over to his train set in the corner of the room and selects a small 'shunter' engine from the middle of the tracks. He puts the train onto the turntable and twists it around manually. There's a lot of clicking and whirring until suddenly a fine beam fires out of the train's lights and illuminates the football pitch in the scenery.

"Activate crowd," commands Grandpa.

The sound of the crowd cheering flies from tiny speakers in the engine's armour.

"Wow Grandpa, that's really cool."

"It's just a prototype but wouldn't it be great if I could project holograms of players for an actual match."

"What like our team?"

"Absolutely, I figure it could be a good tool to use for team talks."

"Do you know how to do that?"

"Err, no." He turns the 'shunter', and the whole picture disappears. "It's a quirky concept, though, don't you think? I could call it the 'training' tool!" He laughs at his own joke.

Grandpa's always developing ideas. I think that's what he does in the bunker down at the vegetable patch. Secret invention plans, that's why it's kept locked and no one else is allowed in.

"Anyway," he claps his hands in the air, "back to business. We need to hatch a plan for Barney Frank to break into the world of football. Put the kettle on."

We decide to use Grandpa's email address to receive the challenges. He'll act as my co-entrant, and I'll be the spokesman. Perfect.

"How about we share our exciting news with the family tonight over a bowl of your mum's spaghetti bolognese?" Grandpa suggests once we've finished.

"Er...yeah, ok." Do I want to tell all of them?

"You don't sound so sure. They'll be thrilled."

"Will they?" I hesitate. "Ok." I can feel Grandpa's examining stare.

***

A strong smell of the bolognese fills my nostrils as Mum lifts the lid on the pan. I'm laying the table in the kitchen when another advert for the 'Premiership's Football Manager Show' blasts out of the TV. Grandpa puts down his newspaper and moves closer to the screen.

My fingers forget how to hold all the cutlery in my hand. Knives and forks tumble noisily onto the table. I feel wobbly. Will it mention me in the advert? When will the show be screened? Do I get to miss school? I hold the back of the chair to steady myself.

"Not that rubbish again," scoffs Dad as he walks into the room. "The average, ordinary bloke isn't going to be able to sort that club out, even for a charity match. It needs a professional. The show's a waste of time."

"Barney *was* going to enter, but he's probably missed the deadline now," pipes Hattie.

Argh! Why does she always have to drop me in it?

This time Dad takes notice. "There's my point," he snorts. "Ridiculous, you'll never get on that show, son, not in a million years. And even if you did well, who's going to listen to a kid?" He empties the contents of a beer can into his tankard and slurps from it noisily. I feel like I've swallowed a load of ice cubes.

Grandpa plonks the water glasses onto the table, which clink as they collide. He peers at me over the rim of his spectacles, putting his forefinger to his lips.

I want to tell Dad, to shout out loud that actually I *have* been chosen, so there!

"Not tonight, Barney," Grandpa murmurs, squeezing my shoulders. My eyes are burning a hole in the table and I'm breathing hard.

"Let's keep it our secret for the moment." Grandpa's calming whisper wraps around me. He's right. For something this important, a life-changing opportunity, I need to concentrate without distractions. I lay out the cutlery and grin to myself as I put Dad's knife and fork the wrong way round on purpose.

Only Grandpa and I know that Barney Frank, the Football Manager is preparing for launch.

9: MAKING THE RIGHT CHOICE

I'm analysing the form of the Premiership players before I change my fantasy league football team. Picking a good team will show that I know what I'm talking about. I reckon the TV people will be watching my every move.

"Bumble." Mum reads from the list over my shoulder. "You should pick Bumble, that's a lovely name."

"You can't pick a player based on his name, that's ridiculous." I roll my eyes at her then return to scanning the list. I click on Zeph Hewson, a Harlimac attacker, hasn't made it past 50 minutes. Too risky.

"Zeph, sounds like zoom, sounds fast. I'm going to buy him later," Hattie butts in, tapping the screen. "He's going to score lots of goals, and I'm going to beat you and Al."

"You *cannot* pick a player based on their name!" I laugh. "If a girl named Winnie trialled for the football team, would you pick her because she might win?"

Hattie screws up her face. "Of course I wouldn't. Winnie's not a fast name." She tosses her mane of messy hair and trots out of the room. At least I should be able to beat my stupid sister in the fantasy league, even if I can't score as many goals as her on the pitch.

***

"Why are you trying to beat Hattie?" Grandpa asks. "Why swim against the tide when you can float along with it?" He's stacking pots by the greenhouse, his cold nose dripping as he works.

"Brothers and sisters always compete," I reply. Grandpa's got a lot of little sayings and sometimes it takes a while for me to work out what he means.

"If you think Hattie is such a good sportswoman, why don't you help make her even better? Or get *her* to help *you*?" Grandpa sprinkles the earth with water.

"Why would I do that?" I splutter, shaking my head and forgetting to mask the horror. What a crazy idea.

I take over the watering. Help Hattie. Hattie Help. The words are gradually working a route through my brain.

"That's it!" I cry. "I'll train Hattie. It'll help me practise for the show."

"Now that could be a good idea," murmurs Grandpa, bending down to grasp a long leafy frond.

"Barney Frank the coach goes into action!" I nod to myself. That sounds good. "They'll have to pick me."

Grandpa chuckles. "Done any coaching before?"

I plonk the watering can down on the path. "Not exactly."

Grandpa begins digging the ground with a fork, grumbling about mice. "Hope my parsnips haven't been affected," he rambles, tugging at the green shoots. Carefully, he eases out of the ground

32

the longest parsnip I've ever seen. "Now look at the size of that. Lovely jubbly." He shakes the parsnip, scattering mud in my freshly gelled hair. I brush away grit with my fingers.

"That'll do for today, Barney. Thanks for your help. Can you just leave this in the kitchen on your way back?"

I sprint across the lawn. Dropping the veg on the side, I dart up the stairs, pulling out a folded piece of paper from my pocket – my first emailed challenge, received this morning. I've been trying not to think about it.

I slam my bedroom door behind me and chuck a handful of my army characters onto the carpet in front of the door. That should slow anyone down trying to enter uninvited. I pull out the bottom drawer of my desk and rummage through a pile of magazines and comics to find the shoebox hidden underneath them. The box is secured with one of Dad's extra-long bootlaces knotted at right angles across the lid like a present. The bow is tied so tight, I have to use my teeth to prize it apart.

I unfold the emailed challenge and lay it out on the floor.

Football Manager Challenge Number One: Describe how to help players increase the number, strength and accuracy of shots on 'target'. You have five days to email your reply with details of practical demonstrations.

My stomach churns as I read the words again. Removing the lid off the box, I fish out my neatly-written copies of my entry to the Premiership's Football Manager Show, along with lots of other notes. I flick through the sheets until I find my original training plans for the Harlimac Harrier. I run my fingers down the lines of writing searching for 'The Fireball'.

Harlimac are definitely in need of this one. I just need to recruit my Harlimac Harrier, and now I know who.

10: THE HARLIMAC HARRIER

I'm grating cheese over my baked beans on toast when the phone rings. That'll be Granny (Dad's mum). She always calls at the same time on the same day each week. Mum picks up the phone, mouths 'Granny' and leaves the kitchen to chat. Hattie and I are alone.

"So…" I pick up my fork. "How about I train you to be a fantastic sports person?" I stir in the cheese, watching it melt, not wanting to look at Hattie. When I risk a glance at her, her food-filled cheeks are ballooning. Before a laugh escapes and she splatters me in tomato sauce, I add, "It's part of my entry to the Premiership Football Manager Show."

"So you *are* entering. I knew it!" She stabs a bean triumphantly. I take a glug of water as a lump of burning hot cheese slips down my throat.

"You'd appear as my successful sporting…um… phenomenon."

Her smug smile tells me she's interested. "You do know that Reggie Hunter is hosting that show?"

"Yes." I didn't, actually, but this is useful information.

"Would I get to meet him?" She leans across the table towards me. Her eyes are so wide I can almost see myself reflected in her eyeballs.

"Possibly." I dangle the bait. She draws back a little. I need to be more positive. "Sure, if we succeed."

"Yes!" She's hooked as soon as the words leave my lips. Reggie is her all-time-favourite footballing star.

I grin and stuff a forkful of beans into my mouth. That was easier than I expected.

"Have you spoken to him?"

"Not yet..." I clear my throat.

"But they've been in touch...his people."

Without waiting for me to answer, Hattie's mouth dives into full motor action, suggesting training drills and competitions she could enter. "We should set some goals. Like for our school to win the Cup and for me to be the top goal scorer." I nod as I work through my tea. "And I want to improve on my tennis. Anything to show off my ball skills. And... and... "

I zone out for a while. What if she's impossible to manage? On and on she goes and we haven't even started training yet. As I scoop up my last baked bean, I can hear Mum's footsteps coming back to the kitchen.

I reach out and grab Hattie's hand. "You can't tell anybody."

She looks up at me and wrinkles her top lip.

Mum is standing just outside, saying her goodbyes to Granny.

"Nothing is certain and anything you say to anyone, even Mum or Dad, could ruin my ... our ... chances," I hiss.

"Do you want a quick chat with the children?" asks Mum.

"Not a word," Hattie whispers, zipping her lips with her fingers.

Mum breaks off the call. "Sorry, kids, Granny had to dash, she's off to a new tap dancing class."

Hattie winks at me.

11: FIRST CHALLENGE

It's four days until the TV show email deadline. I've been working on my fresh ideas, planning a few tasks to set Hattie. Hopefully I can improve her shooting accuracy. I've requested plenty of fresh fruit and vegetables from the kitchen staff (alias Mum); you are what you eat. But I need to make a start with testing out my training exercises. The Harlimac Harrier's shooting skills better be good if she's to beat Al to the position of top scorer.

Today I introduce Hattie to my first drill. Take note, history is about to be made. Barney Frank the football manager is putting his plans into practice.

The aim is to improve shots on goal. I set up three targets for Hattie to shoot at on the football pitch after school. One is my school bag, a big obstacle at close range. Further away is Hattie's bag, a big obstacle at long range. And in between is one of my smelly socks, a small obstacle at mid range. This is going to be the hardest. I tell Hattie that she can't leave until she hits each target four times.

She easily hits my bag four times in a row. I notice that she misses out the sock altogether and starts shooting at her bag, further away. Hitting it only once in four attempts, she begins to complain. "I'm tired."

"Work harder!" I shout, backing towards the targets. "That's what Reggie Hunter would say. If you really want to be a superstar, that is!"

Snarling at me, she swipes the ball. In slow motion I turn to retreat but the deadly torpedo is already on course. A direct hit, at close range. The ball smacks into my bottom. "Ouch!"

"Goodbye, Barney!" Hattie calls. "You can bring my bag home if you want me to keep quiet." She storms off the field, leaving me to collect all the balls.

"Hattie, you can't give up already. I thought you wanted to be the best?" I shout after her, but she doesn't turn around.

What a disaster. My first task, and my striker's given up. I've only got four days left to reply.

***

My sister is suffering mood swings. Actually, I am suffering from Hattie's mood swings. I can't speak, eat or move without her barking at me.

Mum says that I should: "Leave Hattie alone and give her some space, Barney. It's probably puberty." That embarrassing thing they keep insisting on talking about at school.

"I'm exactly the same age and I'm not moody," I complain.

Mum looks at me silently. She walks over to the kitchen door, gently opening and closing it. I know what she's thinking. I do vaguely remember slamming the kitchen door last night after a disagreement with Dad about time spent watching TV, but that was different. I was provoked.

12: HATTIE'S REPORT

I've had the TV show challenge for three days now and have still got nothing to write. My Harlimac Harrier's barely speaking to me and to make matters worse the school reports arrive in the post this morning.

Whilst Hattie and I are having supper we can see Dad's legs sticking out from the armchair at the other end of the lounge diner. He's reading Hattie's report. I watch my sister's eyes dart between her bowl of soup and Dad's armchair. Quietly grunting like a foraging pig, he flicks through the pages.

"Barney!" Mum snaps, over at the hob, as I slurp up my soup. I am trying to distract Hattie, but it isn't working.

Mum glances at Dad. "Top of the class in PE!" she calls out, reminding Dad of Hattie's one good result. I wish I was top of PE.

"You appear to have a concentration problem, Hattie," grumbles Dad. Only the end of his long bristled nose peeps out from the wing of the chair.

Mum turns up the gas, and the soup begins bubbling.

Hattie's head sinks lower over her steaming bowl. She looks at me across the rim of her spoon. "Help me," she mouths, her eyebrows reaching for her fringe.

"How?" I whisper.

She glares at me.

OK. This is my chance to please her then we can start training again.

"Have you got my report, Dad?" I ask. Hattie rolls her eyes. It was all I could think of!

"As I told you earlier, son, you're flying in maths and science but are decidedly average elsewhere." Is that a compliment? I'm not sure I want to be average. I want to be the best.

Hattie kicks me under the table and screws up her nose.

The old armchair creaks as Dad heaves himself up.

"I'm going to mull things over in my office," he informs us, waving the report card in Hattie's direction. "And decide on the consequences."

Ouch!

***

I've got to perfect the shooting practice. The days are ticking by and my response to the TV show grows more urgent every second. I'll impress Dad by being more than an *average* football manager.

My aim is to improve shots on goal by channelling your energy. (I read about this in a book.)

After school, I persuade Hattie to try the shooting task again with a few adjustments. I borrow plastic cups from the school canteen to replace the bags. I wanted to use cones but I don't have any, but these are the right shape, and smaller, which makes it more difficult.

"Hit each cup once," I tell Hattie, placing a few balls by her feet.

Why only once?

a) We don't have all night.

b) I don't want a repeat of the last lesson. I've still got a bruised bum cheek.

As Hattie gets better, I'll increase the number of shots on target.

"Imagine a burning fireball of energy in your belly button," I say.

"Yuk!" she squirms.

I ignore her. "Now you need to send that fireball down through your body." I draw an imaginary line down my leg. "Over your knees, along your shin, into your ankle." I pull my leg back and flex my foot. "And out through your toes as you shoot."

Then I give her a slow-motion demo, rubbing my belly before flinging my arms towards my leg, sending it flying out in front of me. The force is so powerful I nearly fall over.

"You look stupid!" she laughs.

"Try it!" I demand.

The first few attempts are pathetic really. She misses twice, and then slices the ball, sending it spiralling off to the side.

"This is crazy. I want to score goals, not hit plastic cups." She scuffs her shoes into the mud.

"Try again. If you can hit a small cup, you'll be able to smack the target in a football match every time." I throw her the ball and pick up two of the cups.

She pulls at her hair, tying her bunches in a knot.

"Tell you what, let's change tactics," I call, picking up the last cup. I stack the three cups together and place them in the middle of the bench on the side of the sports field. Taking a deep, calming breath, I walk over to Hattie.

"You're aiming at the bench." I hold her head in my hands and turn it to look at the bench. She nods, so at least I know she's listening. "Now imagine Dad is sat on the bench and he's holding your school report on top of the stack of cups." I'm trying to copy the tone of Mum's soothing yoga video.

Hattie's cheeks suck in, and her body shudders. I didn't realise the report issue scared her that much.

"Kick the ball and try to knock the report out of his hands."

I step away.

I can hear her chanting under her breath. "School report, school report, school report."

Explosive! Hattie smashes ball after ball into the stack of cups. Firing the last one so hard that the bench topples over too.

Surely they've got to pick me, this is a fab demonstration for the email challenge. To give your shots strength and accuracy, you need to think of an image to fire at. I know what mine is.

***

Grandpa is really impressed when I run home to tell him.

"You narrate, and I'll type," he says. He clicks on the email from the TV show and sets up a reply page. "In fact, we could try my new narration mode I've developed if you like." He clicks on an icon of a pair of puffy red lips. "Testing, testing, one, two, three." He speaks to the computer. It types back; 'Bonjour Barnaby. Hola, Ciao, Guten

Morgen, Bon Nuit'. "Not quite the response I was expecting. Perhaps we'd better stick to me typing."

"Yeah, I think so too Grandpa."

I tweak a few adjustments to the original task to make it sound more professional, like using cones in a Premiership stadium rather than canteen cups on a school playing field.

"We can't use an image of Dad holding a school report so I was thinking maybe a pay cheque for thousands of pounds."

Grandpa winces. "Does it have to be about money? How about winning something?"

I lean back in the chair whilst I'm thinking. "Winning *Player of the Season!*" I jump forward. Harlimac's striker, Agrovio, could've done with that motivation months ago.

"Perfect. I like it," Grandpa agrees.

I reckon the judges will be impressed too.

13: THE FANTASY LEAGUE

The lead in the fantasy football is nearly mine. Al had been pulling away, but scored poorly last week when his team was hit by injury and suspension. I don't reckon anyone else has a chance of catching us at this stage. It's a head to head for Al and me.

My fingers drum against my lips as I review the players' performances. I want to win, to show the football manager show people that I know what I'm doing. I'll show Dad I'm not average, there's something special about me.

I need consistency, nothing too chancy. I'd like to sign up a Harlimac player, to show my loyalty to the club, but their disastrous season isn't filling me with confidence. Hattie chose one of their attackers and a defender at the beginning of the season and now she's third from bottom in our league. Signing Agrovio, their most experienced attacker, was disastrous. He might have been the Premiership's 'Player of the Season' two years ago, but he hasn't scored in the last ten games. Realising her mistake, she is finally selling him, but she'll be lucky to avoid relegation. I can't believe she still carries his picture in a key ring attached to her pencil case.

"I'm going to take a risk and buy Mac and Bird. Mac very nearly scored last week," Hattie announces, bringing up the information on the screen.

"Are you sure? Bird hasn't scored since November, and Mac dived for that penalty and then missed it." I'm trying to be helpful.

"He didn't dive, he was pushed," she bites back.

"Fell down like a baby if you ask me."

"I didn't ask you, so keep your trap shut. I need big points so it's worth the risk." She taps away at the keyboard. "You should be supporting them otherwise they'll never pick you for that show."

She has a point, but I'm confident in my shooting practice challenge. Hattie keeps talking about using an image to shoot at in this week's match. She's been much less moody too, even though Dad's still *mulling over the consequences* of the school report. I wonder if she's just blocking that out?

I scan the Harlimac list of players up for transfer and plump for Vanson, a solid midfielder. I hope he does the team proud.

14: THE SUPER SUB

The bench is hard under my bum. My studs are stuck in the mud, knees trembling with cold, and I'm desperate for the loo. I knew I should have gone before leaving the changing room. Nobody bothered to pack my sweatshirt or a thermal in my sports kit. My flimsy football top is flapping like a flag across my back as I curl up, trying to shield myself from the weather.

Eddie still gets praise from the sidelines even when he drifts in and out of the game. Diego's hopping from foot to foot, no idea who he should be tackling. Lizzie's boot has become our final defence as she's taken up position at the top of the box, battling against anyone who dares to enter her space.

Erica's spark at the beginning of the game, when she headed in one of Hattie's shots, has been snuffed out. Instead, she plods either side of the half way line, booting the ball as soon as it reaches her foot, without any sort of a plan. Cathy is buzzing up and down the pitch trying to pick up the pieces but she's a bit slow. Surprisingly, 'Hogger Hugh' is flying down the wing, firing balls into the box for Hattie. Sadly, Hattie needs more practice on the shooting drill.

Dad is like a foghorn on the sidelines, drowning out the other parents. Sometimes he's so loud you'd think Hattie was the only player on the pitch.

Our weakness today lies in midfield. I count ten occasions in ten minutes when Vijay collects the ball from one of Erica's wild swipes, takes it up the field, dances about trying a few flashy moves and loses it to the opposition. I want to shout '*pass*' but he won't hear me, and he certainly won't listen.

Coach is trying to be encouraging, but he's losing patience, nervous that we'll concede a goal and lose our one nil lead. "Move right, Angus, cover that gap!"

Angus doesn't react when the dribbler changes direction. The opposition jogs past him across the halfway line.

Al's injury has left us open to attack. Losing such a key player in attack and defence could be our downfall. He sits on the bench beside me, tearing at his short hair. "What's Angus doing? Why doesn't he move to tackle?" he growls.

The dribbler is nearing the box but Lizzie is ready. Eddie tunes in and blocks the path to the left but there is space out right and a winger is pacing down the line.

"We're too one sided," I mutter to Big Barry, who's sat beside me on the bench. "Like there's a giant magnet pulling all our players left."

"A magnet?" Barry queries.

"Yeah, look at all that space we've left open for attack on the right." I point it out.

The dribbler releases the ball for the winger, who's racing to the bottom right-hand corner.

"Don't concede now, the whistle must be about to go." Al drums his knees with his fists. A win is slipping away.

"Barney, you're right, you should be Coach." Barry nudges me.

The winger chips the ball into the box. Darting in, the dribbler collects it. Lizzie doesn't move, Eddie is nowhere to be seen, and the dribbler suddenly has a one-on-one with our goalie. We leap to our feet, fearing the worst. Swooping in, a girl with long, red, wavy hair slides in a tackle, sweeping the ball away from the dribbler's leg and out of play.

"Brilliant!" cries the coach. "Brilliant!"

The whistle blows. We are through to the final!

Leaping about wildly the team fly in to congratulate the girl.

But I'm frozen to the bench. I can't speak because it feels like a lump of apple is stuck in my throat. I daren't blink because my eyes are about to flood.

In the most important match of my footballing life, with my dad watching, the red-haired new girl called Olive, subs me and saves the day.

15: DOUBTS

"We're in the final!" Hattie is singing downstairs.

"My girl set up the only goal." Even in the shower, I can hear Dad, filling Grandpa and Mum in on the game. "A beautiful cross for Erica to header. It was brilliant." I stick my head right under the showerhead to drown out his voice.

Finally warmer and dry, I return to the kitchen where Hattie is still in her kit.

"Back of the net!" Dad sticks his hand up for Hattie to high five.

"Does this mean I'm not in trouble any more?" she says with a sickly smile.

Dad frowns. Bad move Hattie. "No, we still need to talk about that report." Dad pauses. Hattie's smile fades. "But not now."

"I've made you a hot chocolate, Barney, to warm you up." I take it from Mum, sit down and clamp my hands around my Harlimac mug. Hattie is twirling and prancing about the kitchen.

"Scrappy game though." At least Dad realises that too. "Shame you were subbed, Barney." He looks over at me, his lips all twisted up. What can I say? I'm gutted. I take a gulp of my hot chocolate.

"All that spinning, Hattie, you're making me dizzy," says Grandpa.

"Come and sit down." Mum catches Hattie mid spin. "Well done. How exciting that your school's in the final." She gives my arm a squeeze too. I try a weak smile.

"If it wasn't for that new girl in the team, things could've been a lot different." Dad shakes his head.

Beware, this is my replacement you're talking about, Dad.

I concentrate on the Harlimac club emblem painted on my mug; it's a red kite in flight. If only I could spread my wings and fly away then I wouldn't have to listen to Dad banging on.

"She made an outstanding tackle right at the end to stop them equalising. You should've seen it."

"That good?" asks Grandpa.

"Grandpa, it was amazing," Hattie adds.

I don't say anything.

"Come on, I think it's time you showered and got out of this dirty kit, Hattie." Mum pushes Hattie up off her lap. "Look I've got a wet patch on my trousers now." They both laugh. Hattie skips out of the kitchen.

"I'm going to my shed, I've got a few things to sort out." Dad takes his teacup to the sink and then disappears out of the back door.

"Barney, do you want to come and help me with the trains?" Grandpa asks.

I don't move.

"I could really do with your help." Grandpa leans across the table and nudges my hand. He winks, tilting his head towards the annex staircase.

"All right," I sigh.

"Sorry I couldn't watch today, Barney. I'd have been there if it wasn't for this damn cold." Grandpa pulls a handkerchief from his pocket and wipes his nose. "You fed up?" He asks as we reach the top of the stairs. I shrug. "Aren't you excited about being in the final?" Grandpa opens the door to his annex. I shrug again. He looks directly at me. "Is it because you were subbed?" I feel my bottom lip wobbling. "And because that girl saved the day? Your replacement."

I nod. My eyes are filling up again. Why do I keep crying? I'm supposed to be growing up.

"How can I be a coach when I can't even make the team? Dad's right, I'm not good enough." I sniff.

"Ah no, come on, your dad doesn't even know you're entering. He wouldn't think that."

"Wouldn't he?"

Grandpa puts his arm around my shoulders and guides me over to his computer. "You look at this," he suggests, tapping away at the keyboard. "Some of the best football managers never played top professional football."

On the screen he shows me big names that never played in the Premiership but still manage in it.

"You don't have to be skilful with the ball to be skilled at reading the game."

Maybe he's right. "I don't need to be the top goal scorer to work out how to score the goals," I suggest.

"Absolutely."

53

I sit back, twiddling my thumbs. Maybe I can do this.

"What qualifications do you think I'd need to be a football manager?" I ask him.

"Oh well, um … hardworking," he says, handing me a block of wood and a piece of sandpaper from a pile beside his railway. "I need that sanding down to the line, it's going to be part of the scenery."

Landscaped into the corner of his sitting room, Grandpa's railway set has grassy hills, woods, tunnels and a row of shops.

I start rubbing the paper up and down against the wood. Grandpa opens a tiny pot of paint and begins decorating another chunk of wood, turning it into a rock face.

"Do you think I would make a good coach?" I ask. "Honestly."

Grandpa frowns, his jaw moving silently while he thinks. I manage to sand all the way down to the marker before he speaks.

"There's nothing like your youthful enthusiasm and endless energy," he says with a chuckle.

"I'm being serious," I remind him as I hand back the wood.

"Serious, of course." He blows away the fine layer of sawdust and puts it next to his paint pots. "I guess you have lots of fresh ideas that are different to anyone else's. Unique!"

"Yes," I agree. "Fresh ideas," I repeat to myself.

"So!" Grandpa says suddenly, hitting the computer mouse. "What are we going to do about this?" An email appears on the screen.

My arms prickle as I read the email. It's our second challenge sent from Broadcasting Base.

Football Manager Challenge Number Two – Demonstrate how to keep your players fit enough for a ninety-minute match. You have four days to reply. Details of exercise plans are advised.

"We're still in the competition," I yelp.

16: CHALLENGE NUMBER TWO

Grandpa believes getting the right amount of sleep and a good balanced diet are both important for this next challenge. I think they want more examples of how to improve a player's fitness, not just make them feel healthy and awake. We've spent over an hour discussing it.

"So we're agreed on a middle ground," Grandpa says. "Providing she gets enough sleep and eats well, then we can devise a series of drills to improve Hattie's fitness levels."

"Remember she won't be playing for ninety minutes. Our matches are only an hour long, Grandpa."

"Sure." Over the top of his glasses Grandpa reads through my notes again. What's the point of wearing glasses if you're not going to look through them? He taps one line. "You don't think this is too much to expect?"

"Be ready to react," I read out. "No, she needs to be fit."

Grandpa bites his bottom lip with his false teeth.

"Well, we can build her up to that level gradually if she's struggling." I'm giving in a bit, just to keep Grandpa happy.

"So which are you going to test out first?" he asks.

"The stamina one."

"Is that the food one?"

"It offers food rewards, if that's what you mean."

"I see." He raises his eyebrows. It would be so much easier if he just agreed with me all the time.

"It's good to offer incentives, Grandpa, that's why professionals are paid so much."

"Too much, in my opinion." I knew he'd say that.

"Let's meet again tomorrow evening after I've tried out the first drill. We only have four days to reply."

"Roger that." Grandpa salutes me.

***

My aim is to increase stamina whilst practising a skill. I've chosen dribbling. Stamina's a big word I heard sports reporters talking about on the telly. Basically, it's about how long a player can keep going.

Today I act as Hattie's pacemaker. I space eight small bowls in two rows running from the patio to the fence, four for me and four for Hattie.

In each of Hattie's bowls I put an increasing number of grapes, from one in the first bowl to four in the last. They're increasing, because that adds an extra incentive to finish the task.

In each of my bowls I put chocolate buttons, until I've emptied a whole packet.

The idea of the task is to sprint, whilst dribbling a football, from the patio to the fence and back, collecting treats from a bowl each time you complete a sequence.

Collecting grapes in her pocket, Hattie waits until she finishes the task, in less than 3 minutes, before eating the incentives.

I begin eating the minute I pick up my first treat. By the time I reach the third bowl of chocolate, I'm not enjoying it quite so much. I choke, but jog on with a sickly taste at the back of my throat.

"Ouch! I've got a stitch." I clutch my tummy. Ugh I feel sick!

I can't use this. What am I going to do now?

17: PROBLEMS

Grandpa and I meet again. "I don't think we can use the stamina drill."

"Why's that?"

"It didn't work very well," I admit.

"I thought you said that Hattie completed the task in three minutes."

"Yeah, but she isn't any fitter because of it. Besides, being fit for three minutes doesn't mean you'll last ninety."

"True." Grandpa squashes his teabag with a spoon, lifts it out of his mug and drops it in the bin. "I like a good brew, one that's left for a long time."

"We could do with leaving Hattie to stew," I say. "Give her a drill that really pushes her to her limits."

"Maybe a few stretches and a feet-blistering jog around the park in big boots, like in my army days." Hm. Grandpa's ideas might need updating.

"What about a mini marathon with sweat-busting exercises every four hundred metres?" I suggest.

"After every lap of a running track?"

"Yeah, push-ups, squats!"

"That's tough. Remember she's only twelve," he warns.

"Obviously I'll make it easier for Hattie. She can do the exercises every two hundred metres, that's only halfway round a track."

Grandpa whistles.

"Still too tough?"

"Perhaps we are looking at this the wrong way, Barney. A player needs to be consistently good throughout an entire game. That's not just about being able to sprint around the whole time."

"Huh. Do you think it's not just about fitness then? More about staying focused and alert for a whole game?" Eddie could definitely do with that sort of training.

Grandpa tips his ear to his shoulder and I know he agrees. This is the route we need to follow.

***

The aim is to keep your focus over time.

Hattie is about to find out that you can't just be good here and there; it's about *consistency* – being the best again and again...always.

"Every hour, upon the hour, between 9am and 6pm, you'll be expected to perform keepie-ups for thirty seconds with the football," I instruct.

"Easy," she says.

"Without letting the ball drop. Otherwise you start again."

"Ugh!" She snorts like a pig.

"You may stop and rest as soon as you manage thirty seconds without dropping the ball. The time is 8.59am. You may begin in 5,4,3,2,1...now!"

As the day goes on, I think the practice will improve her skills, but she'll get tired and make more mistakes. This is a scientific test.

At first Hattie concentrates hard and completes the sets with ease. Late morning, her confidence is soaring and she even sings during the task. Early afternoon, the mistakes begin trickling in, and she takes longer and longer to complete the task.

"This is an excellent demonstration of tiredness affecting performance," Grandpa comments as he visits the training session mid afternoon.

Errors are flying in thick and fast. She only manages to keep the ball up for four or five nudges at a time. It takes half an hour to finish the three-o'clock task, which means little time to rest before starting again at four

"But is it actually improving her fitness?" I wonder.

Half past four, tea mug in hand, Dad walks out onto the decking.

Hattie draws a deep breath as Dad interrupts her longest set yet.

"Can I suggest a change of style?"

She glares back at him.

"Dad, we're in the middle of something important here," I protest. He's ruining my scientific test.

"Let me demonstrate." Dad places the ball down and rolls each trouser leg up to his knees. Dad may well have been his school's top centre forward, but those days are long gone, along with leather-

61

laced balls. He hasn't done any keepie-ups for near on two decades.

"You ought to stand up straight, and keep looking ahead. Don't watch the ball." He lifts his hand up to his eye and points his forefinger out in front of him. "Let your legs do all the work."

"That's not how we've been taught at school."

"I was nearly professional, Barney," he reminds me.

How could I forget with all his polished trophies on display? But Dad's playing days are a distant memory. The only regular exercise he gets is walking from the front door to the car. It's quite sad.

He hooks the ball up off the decking with his foot, which is impressive. He nudges the ball up once, twice, three times. Grinning, he says, "you see, this is how you do it."

He's up to ten. Showing off, he throws his shoulders back. "Aargh!" he yells, grabbing the back of his thigh as his left foot slips on a wet leaf. Off balance, his right foot kicks out and his body crashes onto the decking. I can feel the vibration. Meanwhile, the ball shoots off, high over the fence. The crash of breaking glass tells us it's landed in next-door's greenhouse.

Test abandoned.

"My leg, my leg!" Dad wails like a baby. "Fetch some ice, I've pulled something," he moans.

Hattie races off to the kitchen.

I walk over to where Dad is crouched and look down at him. For a second I feel very tall.

"Get your mother, Barney. I'm injured," he moans.

Serves you right, I want to say.

"Quick, Barney, go!"

I hesitate. Is he going green? "Mum!" I yell, and run towards the house.

***

After paying a small fortune to Mr Angry next door, Dad rigs up a net for us to practise under. He spends a lot of time moaning about his bad leg. I'm not sure how long Dad's handiwork will stay standing. I'm worried about getting trapped inside, but Hattie loves the enormous fruit cage. She's out practising every evening under the patio spotlight.

.

***

"Dad ruined the focus drill," I complain to Grandpa. I pick up a train and rest it carefully on the tracks.

"I don't think he meant to, he was only trying to help. Besides, he doesn't even know why you are training Hattie." Grandpa is studying one of the carriages under a magnifying glass, trying to work out why its wheels won't move.

"We only have one more day before we need to reply." I twist the dial on the control box, and the train sets off out of the station and into a tunnel. I've only recently been allowed to work the trains. Grandpa's very protective over them and has never really forgotten the time I caused a multiple pile up by twisting all the control dials at once. I was only six at the time. "We'll have to try out *Ready to React*."

Grandpa stops looking at the broken carriage and stares at me. "Is that wise?"

"It's our only chance, tomorrow afternoon." I spin the control dial too fast, the train flies out of the tunnel and narrowly misses a coal truck on the other line but slams into the back of the 'shunter'. The shunter's lights flick on and the sound of the crowd cheering fills the room. Oops.

"Interesting," says Grandpa. "I never knew the projection would work off the turntable. I wonder how I managed that?"

18: INTERFERENCE

Dad is making a slow recovery. Like a bad smell that won't go away, he turns up to watch our next training session.

"This is a great idea of yours, Barney, helping Hattie ahead of the big final." I suppose he's at least crediting me with something, even though he doesn't really know what's going on. He hobbles off down to the shed, right in the middle of my training ground.

I try to ignore him as I explain the list of exercises Hattie is to complete. 'Ready to React' is an exercise regime I've devised to keep players fit.

This test requires a mixture of sprints, dribbling with the ball, squats, sit-ups and press-ups. I want to make it an hour long, the same length as our game, but Grandpa suggests we start with forty minutes and build up gradually. I've colour coded the instruction cards that I hold up to help Hattie identify what exercise she must do. For instance, 'sit ups' are written in red and 'squats' in blue. Every so often I fling in a 'Chase the player' card, which means she has to race to the fence and back.

"Think of it as marking your player; don't let them get away," I tell her.

Before we start, I time her over the sprint length and then show her a new running technique that I found on the Internet, keeping her knees up high.

Hattie races past the shed as Dad emerges carrying a padded garden chair.

"Jog back to allow your body to rest," I call out. But Dad catches her arm as she passes the shed and hands over the garden chair. Of course she carries it for him. He limps along behind.

She puts the chair up on the patio for Dad, then steps back onto the grass and looks to me for instruction. I click the stopwatch as I hold up a 'Chase the player' card to start her off again.

"Keep your knees up!" I remind her.

She's fast. I hold up a 'Press ups' card as soon as she returns.

We have been going for ten minutes when Dad suddenly starts firing extra instructions. "Use your arms to propel yourself!"

"Dad, you're interfering, it's confusing Hattie." I try to breathe deeply.

"Nonsense, son, she needs more direction."

I grind my teeth and hold up a new card, changing the exercise to dribbling between cones.

Legs cocooned in a blanket, Dad snuggles into his padded garden chair as the sky darkens and the wind picks up. "Control the ball! Keep it on your feet!" he bellows.

I feel like I might explode. I pull out my phone and scroll down to find some inspirational music. The 'Star Wars' theme tune blasts out of the speakers, and Dad is silenced for a while.

Half an hour later and Hattie is flagging. Her sprint times peaked at twenty-two minutes, but are now slowing. I suspect there's too many sprints, much more than in a proper game, and too few rest periods.

"Fitness, Hattie! Come on!" shouts Dad, spraying the patio with digestive biscuit crumbs. "Fetch me another biscuit to dip in my tea will you, Barney."

"We're just about to finish, Dad." I decide to stop earlier than planned. It's cold sitting out here watching.

"What? No, there's far more training she needs to do. I'll keep an eye on Hattie, you fetch the biscuits…and another cup of tea, this one's cold." He hands me his mug and ushers me inside. "Keep going, girl!" he bellows.

I stand at the kitchen window watching my poor sister complete an exhausting stream of squats and sprints whilst the kettle boils beside me. It'll be all right, I guess, if I give the same drill for a sixty-minute session to a professional player. They should be able to cope with more than Hattie anyway. I know it's tough, and it needs to be for them to improve, but perhaps it's too much for a twelve year old.

"Oh, are you making tea?" Mum arrives back from the supermarket. "I'd love a cuppa." She smiles, carrying shopping bags into the kitchen. Then she clocks Hattie puffing and panting like a hound at the bottom of the garden. She dumps the bags on the floor and storms out of the back door.

"That's it!" she yells, stomping off down the garden. "Training is over!"

Hattie slumps into a pile on the grass, amongst the worm casts.

"Upstairs for a bath, young lady." Mum pulls Hattie up by the hand. "Really, what on earth do you think you were doing to the girl?" Mum's voice rises by a couple of octaves and quite a few decibels.

"She's fine. Needs toughening up," Dad protests. "You fuss too much."

Mum looks like she's about to breathe fire. Sweeping back up the garden towards the patio clutching Hattie's shoulders, Mum ignores Dad's objections. As they come level on the patio, Dad starts to ease himself out of the chair.

"She is not a machine!" blasts Mum. In a swift and not entirely accidental movement, Mum sweeps her foot under Dad's bad leg as she passes. He yelps, collapsing back onto the chair.

"Oh stop making a fuss!" she snaps before disappearing inside.

19: RESPONSE

Under my door this evening, Hattie shoves a formal complaint.

Dear Coach

After the heavy training, my whole body is aching so much that even a tortoise could beat me.

Yours seeking compensation, Hattie the Superstar

I reply:

Dear Superstar in training

> *You should have done a proper warm down of stretches when you came in. You should also avoid listening to other people's bad coaching advice.*

> *Yours The 'Free' Coach (i.e. no charge)*

I think that gets the message across.

***

I patch together an email to send to the Premiership's Football Manager Show, combining the *Ready to React* and *Focus* drill. I increase the 'Chase the Player' card into a fifty-metre dash and combine it with the 'keepie ups' as one of the tasks on the instruction cards. Grandpa thinks it's important to explain the logic behind the drills, so I do that too. I hope they understand all my instructions and reasoning. I wish Grandpa would let me in his secret bunker, and perhaps we could invent something even more exciting. I write a final note about the importance of sleep and a good balanced diet in helping the body recover and maintain fitness levels.

Then I get into bed and wait for sleep to rescue me from the agony of not being the best footballer, and probably not being a good coach either, because I can't even stop my dad interfering.

What will I ever be great at? Anything? Or am I destined to be average, just like Dad said.

There's a rustling outside. I sit up quickly to see a piece of paper being posted under my door. I jump out of bed.

Opening the note I read:

Dear Coach

I am getting faster and stronger. I will be top goal scorer. And I don't think Mum will be letting Dad get involved again any time soon.

Thanks for helping me.

The Harlimac Harrier.

I fold the note into four and hide it away in my secret box.

"Sleep," I yawn, huddling under the duvet. Time for my great mind to recover.

20: VANSON

There's a knock at my bedroom door. I know it's Dad, he's the only one who stomps up the stairs. He's been to the last game of the season with Grandpa this evening. I wasn't allowed to go because it's a school night. Mum's house rules.

"Barney, you still awake?" His head peeps around the door. I turn the bedside light on and lean back on my elbows.

"You'll never guess what." He wanders in perching on the end of the bed.

"What?" I say.

"Harlimac actually won! In the last five minutes Vanson set up a great chance for Agrovio from the edge of the box. Agrovio falls in a tackle and is given a penalty. We're still in the Premiership next season. Can you believe it?" He clenches both fists.

"That's great, Dad. Did Agrovio take the penalty too?"

"No, Vanson."

"Vanson! The mid-fielder?"

"Yeah, it was a great shot, keeper dived the wrong way." Dad pushes himself up. "Anyhow, you'd better get some rest, Hattie's already asleep. I'll see you in the morning. Goodnight."

"Night."

He strolls out and closes the door. I flick my light off and flop back onto the pillow. Typical, Vanson scores the minute I sell him. Then I remember that Al bought Vanson this week. I sneak over to my iPad and quickly check on the fantasy league. The screen lights up the room and it doesn't take long to find out the result. My title bid is over. I'm runner up, beaten by Al. I bet he'll be gloating tomorrow.

I flop back into bed. I've lost the fantasy league race. My last entry to the Premiership's Football Manager Show probably isn't good enough either. I turn over, I can't sleep. Think positive, I tell myself. At least no news means I haven't been chucked out just yet, hopefully.

21: THE CHEAT

"Dad!" I race downstairs as Dad arrives back from work. "Have you seen the papers?" I ask as I follow him into the kitchen. "Agrovio dived for that penalty." I turn over the newspaper on the table and direct him to the picture spread across the back page.

He glances at it only briefly and shakes his head. "Nah! It's difficult to see from that angle."

"But Dad the reporter has watched it back in slow motion. Look here, it reads: the defender withdraws his foot and never touches Agrovio's leg."

Dad starts opening his mail. "We got a penalty son and we won. That's all I need to know." He puts the letters in his back pocket and walks over to the sideboard. "Harlimac are staying in the Premiership." He grins, picking up several trophies out of the cabinet. "I'm going to polish my trophies in my office." He leaves the room.

"But he's a cheat." I'm left talking to no one but myself.

22: PREMIERSHIP TURF

"Why haven't we heard anything? It's been four days," I say to Grandpa as we step off the bus.

"They've got a lot to consider." A snail moves faster than Grandpa is walking.

"How long does it take to decide if a drill works or not?" I clatter a tin can along the gutter.

"They'll have hundreds of entries to sift through."

How's mine going to stand out? If only we'd sent a postal entry, we could've printed it on shiny gold paper.

"They could at least let us know if we're still in the running."

Grandpa shakes his head. "Patience is not one of your finest qualities, Barney."

I boot the can across the road. "Al's brother reckons that our school coach didn't get through because he won't speak about it any more."

Grandpa shrugs. "Just you think about yourself, don't focus on what your competitors are doing. Now, we need to get in the mood," Grandpa announces as he stops outside the stadium gates. "Imagine the stamping boots as the players run down the tunnel, the roar of the crowd as the teams emerge onto the pitch, the squeal of the referee's whistle."

It's difficult to get 'in the mood' when the place is empty. The stadium walls tower above us, casting a cold shadow across the car park. Besides, what are we getting in the mood *for*, exactly?

"Shame we couldn't get a ground tour organised," I sigh.

Grandpa grins. "Well, just so happens that I know a man from the bowls club, who has a sister whose husband's friend helps cut the grass. Morning, Billy." Grandpa waves to a man wearing dungarees and gardening gloves.

"Really?" What's Grandpa got planned?

"Morning, lads. You wanna come and watch me prepare the pitch?" says the man as he waddles over to the gate with a bunch of keys.

"Grandpa, are you kidding me?" I squeeze his hand in mine.

"Oh, I don't joke about important matters like lawn mowing."

I'm about to tread on the turf of the Premiership. I can't wait to tell Al and Hattie.

"You can walk on this end but not on the striped side where I've already started mowing."

Even Grandpa's feet are dancing.

We stand at the corner flag, looking out across the bright green pitch.

"Your dad would love stripes like this on his lawn. I think we ought to take our shoes off Barney." Grandpa slips one shoe off and holds on to my shoulder as he pulls at his sock.

"What for?"

"Feel the turf on your toes." I kick off my trainers and tug at my socks as Grandpa's rolling his trousers up to his knees. This is crazy.

I notice a man and woman in overalls painting the dugout and a person in one of the glazed boxes polishing the window. The seats in the enormous stadium appear to curve up and hug the pitch from this angle. I feel about the size of a pea in a bag of watermelons.

Grandpa steps onto the Harlimac pitch. I follow. The cold grass blades tickle my toes.

"They are not just grounds men in charge of this pitch. They're scientists who understand the soil." Holding my arm, Grandpa gets down on his knees and looks across the top of the grass blades. "Perfect. This pitch is an art form, Barney, not a weed in sight," he tells me, using my arm as a winch to pull him back up. "Now, who can say that gardening is boring when it's so important?"

"Bit different to our school pitches, sloping and peppered with rabbit holes. We're lucky if we get nets in the goalposts." I walk over to the fresh white nets in the goal.

The man on the tractor mower at the other end of the pitch waves to us. Grandpa salutes him back. Another man begins a slow walk pushing the line painter.

"Everything plays a part in the team's success, Barney. People take it for granted that the players run out onto a perfect pitch in clean kit and polished boots."

I'd never thought of it like that before.

Grandpa fakes shooting at the goal and I fling myself into the air between the posts. "Barney Frank saves the day!"

"The crowd goes wild!"

"The team race to congratulate him." I wave my arms above my head. I can see all the guys high-fiving me: Al, Hattie, even Eddie. We'd never get to play on a pitch like this. Well, maybe Al will one day. I hope he doesn't forget me. I'll forgive him for all the bragging he's done about the fantasy league win.

"Barney." Grandpa jogs over to join me. "Let's take a selfie, you and me in goal." He holds out his phone and captures us waving from the Harlimac nets.

Before we leave, Grandpa quietly slips something into my hand. "Keep it safe, a lucky charm for the final."

I peep into my cupped hands to see a blade of fresh green grass: Harlimac FC Premiership turf.

23: GRANDPA'S SHOCK

The bus arrives late, just as it starts raining. We hop aboard, and Grandpa's phone bleeps. He fumbles with his coat pocket, trying to pull it out. I watch a lady on the pavement struggling to get her umbrella up in the sudden downpour.

"Lucky the bus arrived when it did," I remark. Grandpa doesn't reply. I lay my head against his shoulder. "Thanks for taking me to the ground, Grandpa."

Something's wrong. He's not responding.

I twist my head up to look at his face. "I love football," I say. "I love being part of a team, even if I can't be on the field. I've decided that I'll just enjoy being there."

But Grandpa's face is white. He takes a deep breath in, his lips quivering. I jolt away from him, sitting upright, staring at him.

He lifts the phone in his hand, pointing the screen towards me.

Barnaby Frank, congratulations! You are through to the first round of filming for The Premiership's Football Manager Show.

We're both jigging up and down like little kids needing a pee. Looking at each other, unable to speak. Hamster-like squeaks and squeals are all we can manage. The lady on the seat next to us shuffles away, pulling her shopping closer.

Grandpa tugs a handkerchief from his pocket to wipe his weepy eyes. I read the email again and again, just to check.

A letter will be sent today confirming the details.

We're so excited that we nearly miss our stop.

24: TELLING MUM

Mum yawns as she puts a teapot and a plate of cookies in front of Grandpa and me on the kitchen table.

"I couldn't get to sleep last night." She sits down at the head of the table between us. "So, what did you want to talk to me about?" she asks, pouring the tea.

Grandpa raises his hairy eyebrows and tilts his head. We've decided to let Mum in on our football show filming secret. I wiggle my eyebrows back at Grandpa, as I really can't think what to say, especially since my mouth is full of cookie. He winks. I stare at Mum but still can't speak.

"Barney…" Grandpa tips his head to the other shoulder.

I want to yell, 'I know!' but when I open my mouth nothing comes out.

Is this stage fright already? Why can't I just tell her? But what if she gets angry or thinks I'm crazy or, even worse, what if she's embarrassed by me? Maybe she agrees with Dad and thinks I'm just ordinary.

Mum yawns again, blinking, and looks from me to Grandpa then back to me. "Barney, what have you done?"

Should I have admitted my age on the entry form? It didn't ask for it and the competition rules never mentioned an age limit. So technically I haven't done anything wrong.

"Come on, own up."

"I entered the Premiership's Football Manager Show on TV," I mumble. Now I'm for it.

"Blimey! I wasn't expecting that." She virtually drops her mug onto the table. I lean away, waiting for the lecture. Her shoulders start bouncing and I realise she's giggling.

"What's so funny?" I ask.

"Nothing," she grins, "I'm proud of you." She pats my hand. "I think it's very sweet that you've tried." I snatch my hand away. I'm not five years old.

"I've got through to the next round," I announce just as she takes a sip of tea. She starts choking and tries to swallow as I carry on talking. "Grandpa's entering with me and we have to go to London next week for filming."

Mum's smile evaporates, leaving a hole so wide that I can almost see her tonsils. "How… what… ?" she stammers. Then she turns on Grandpa and growls. "Did you put him up to this?"

Grandpa leans forward and spreads his knobbly fingers on the table. He starts to say something.

"I entered without anyone's help," I blurt. I don't want Grandpa taking the blame, especially since he's now my entry key. "Well, actually, the entry form never asked my age or anything." I think it's important for her to know. "I just forgot to write Barnaby Junior so Grandpa picked up the letter."

I seem to have cast a spell over Mum, she's silent, opening and closing her mouth.

"Have a sip of tea, love," Grandpa suggests. Then he takes command like I hoped he would. "Let me explain how this will work…"

I flop back into my chair. As he waffles on, movement returns to Mum's face.

"Of course," I drag my attention back to Grandpa's voice, "to help Barney with his nerves, I think it's best we keep this a secret between the three of us just now," he says. I nod furiously.

"Well." She sucks in a deep breath and looks at me. "I don't like keeping secrets from Dad and Hattie."

Well Hattie knows I've entered, I'm just not telling her about the filming coz she'd refuse to let me go without her, especially if Reggie Hunter's going to be there.

"Please," I mouth, hoping that she can read my lips. I can tell there's going to be a condition.

"But if you think it will help…"

"Definitely," I assure her.

"OK, just for now. But if you're going to be on the television…" I knew it! What's she going to make me do? "We'd better go shopping, Barney."

"Shopping? What for?" My nose wrinkles.

"To buy you some smart clothes." She squeezes my hand.

"Do we have to?"

"If my boy's going to be on TV, he's got to look good."

I suppose it's a small sacrifice to keep her quiet.

———

25: PREPARATIONS

"Hi, I'm Barney Frank, Football Manager," I announce, staring at the crack in the corner of my ceiling, where a skinny-legged spider is spinning a web. I need to perfect my introduction for the TV show. The days are flying by and I want to be sure I'm ready for filming. I could do with a deeper voice.

I try again. "Hey, Barney Frank, Football Manager." That's wrong, I sound like an American chat-show host. I try resting my chin on my chest to give myself several chins instead of one. I see my reflection in the mirror.

"Hello!" I sound just the same, but now I look stupid. This isn't working.

***

"I bought an outfit for the TV show." Grandpa waves a green plastic bag in my face. "I'll put it on," he says, disappearing into his bedroom. I make myself comfortable in his small sitting room, flicking through a few of his train magazines.

"What do you think of this?"

Turning around, I'm dazzled by a glittery, golden tracksuit.

How can I be honest without being rude? "Er … Wow!"

"Wow, exactly," Grandpa agrees, dusting off his lapels. "Grab their attention."

"Uh-huh."

"See how it shimmers in the light when I move." Grandpa waves an arm under the desk lamp. "All those studio lights will catch it."

"Blinding!"

"Barney, they won't be able to keep their eyes off me. Look at you, you're transfixed already."

Actually I feel a headache coming on from the glare.

"Barney, are you up there?" Mum calls, her footsteps clipping up the stairs. "We need to go shopping!"

I'm trapped. Mum appears at the doorway, takes one look at Grandpa and exclaims, "Blimey, Dad, what on earth are you wearing?"

"Eye-catching isn't it?" he beams.

***

"Mum." I approach this conversation carefully.

We are walking through our local shopping centre, heading for the department store.

"Yes, Barney?" Unfortunately, she's more interested in a pair of blue high-heeled shoes. She stops and stares through the shop window.

"I know that we're on a 'buy Barney an outfit' mission."

"Uh-huh." Is she even listening?

"Well I was just wondering whether we might pick up something for Grandpa, too. Something similar to my outfit, maybe?"

She turns to me and smiles, showing off her perfectly straight teeth, which I did not inherit. "You mean you don't want to go to the show looking like an oversized glitter ball?"

"No!" I say, my cheeks burning at the idea.

With one arm she pulls me close. "I'm sure we can find something a little more suitable."

Phew! Thank goodness for Mum.

"Barney," she says. "You've no idea how difficult it is for me to keep such an exciting secret." She bends her neck to whisper in my ear. "I want to tell *everybody* that my boy is going to be on the Premiership's Football Manager Show."

Mum has a way of making you feel very special.

"Now let's get shopping." Her painted fingernails drag me into a store.

***

"What if I get stage fright?" I ask as Mum pulls at the pink shirt, holding up a navy jumper against it. "I'm not sure about the pink." I screw up my nose.

"Try this." She hands me a pale blue shirt and pulls the curtain across, continuing to offer advice. "I've never been on stage, but I did blow up once in a table tennis final."

"What do you mean you blew up? Can you even play table tennis?"

"I was county champion, Barney."

I grab the curtain and stick my head out. "Were you?" She nods. "But you never said."

"Don't look so shocked. I have an amazing back-hand slice." Mum demonstrates what looks more like a karate chop to me.

"Where are all your trophies?"

"In a box in the loft somewhere, probably. I don't keep them polished in a cabinet if that's what you're asking."

Am I the only one in the family who is trophy-less? I carry on changing.

"Did Dad really win all those football trophies?" I pause as I wrestle with the tiny shirt buttons. "Al's mum buys him a trophy each year if he doesn't win player of the season because she says he deserves it." Mum doesn't comment. "She even gets it engraved with his name."

"Do you think Granny bought some of Dad's trophies?" Mum laughs.

"Did she?" I ask hopefully, pulling back the curtain, but Mum's more interested in my new clothes.

"This blue shirt suits you better." She walks around me, fiddling with the collar and pulling at the sleeves. "Looks smart, especially with these cufflinks. I don't think you'll need a jumper under the studio lights."

Just the mention of studio lights makes my mouth go dry. "So what happened when you blew up?" I ask.

"Well, I'd been Junior County Champion for four years running and was in the semis at the nationals." She picks up the navy jumper and brushes off some fluff. "I had to play a girl from a neighbouring county. I'd played her lots of times before and beaten her every time. I thought it would be an easy win. I was a game up and decided to try out a new serve. Stupid really," she says. "It was my last chance to become national champion as a junior." She ushers me back into the fitting room and draws the curtain. "Get changed, Barney." She carries on, her voice sounding sad and distant behind the curtain. "The serve didn't work, but I kept trying as my coach said I'd need to use it to win in the final. Losing point after point, I left it too late to change back. I let my opponent get too far ahead. I never got to the final."

I change quickly and nip out of the dressing room. Mum is delving about in her handbag, her face turned away.

"So you never became National Champion?"

"No," she says quietly, dabbing at her nose with a tissue. "I played for another year at senior level, but then I started work and I was so busy that I didn't have time for all the practising." She zips up her bag and turns to me. "You have to believe in yourself enough to win." She lifts my chin with her forefinger. "But not so much that you forget your opponents are good too. It's a fine balance." As I hand over the blue shirt, she kisses me on the head. "I'm very proud of you, Barney Frank."

26: MOTIVATING

Sitting with your class notes in front of you on the desk doesn't mean that you're learning what's written on them. Particularly if, like Hattie, you've got a set of threads in your hand and you're weaving a bracelet whilst also bouncing a football between your feet.

The front door slams. Dad's back from work. Hattie jumps and kicks the ball under the bed. She chucks the threads into her desk drawer, puts her elbows on the desktop, sinks her head into her hands and starts fiddling with her hair. Heavy footsteps clump up the stairs. One hand drops to trace the line of words across the page. Hattie mumbles as she reads.

Time to move away from the crack in Hattie's door, where I've been spying on her. She still hasn't had the consequences chat with Dad yet.

***

"What song would you play if you wanted to win a game?" I ask Mum as I help with the washing up.

"To motivate me, you mean?"

"Yeah, I want to help Hattie prepare for the final." I rub my itchy nose with my wrist and get a mouth full of soapy bubbles.

"Is this to help with your football manager thing?" she whispers. Nobody else is in, so I don't know why she's being so secretive.

"Sort of." I don't want to admit that it's not just because I'm a super caring brother.

"That's a tricky one. Hattie likes Little Mix, *Wings are made to fly*," she suggests. I hate that song, probably because Hattie plays it constantly.

"But what would *you* like?" I want something different, a new angle.

She dries three cups before she replies. "*Heroes* by William Joseph, a really moving piece." Mum pretends to play a keyboard, throwing her head around. "You've got to feel the music."

"Was that the one played at the London Olympics?"

"No, that's *Heroes* by David Bowie, this is an instrumental piano piece."

"Hmm, how about something with words, that has a meaning." I pull out the plug and peel off the yellow rubber gloves.

She spends ages, polishing the same glass until it sparkles. Finally, she comes out with, "you mean something like *We are the Champions* by Queen or *Gold* by Spandau Ballet? Though I'm not sure that's got anything to do with winning." She scratches her head. "But maybe it's like a gold medal. Check it out in my collection." She starts singing, then hums - she obviously doesn't know all the words.

***

evening, I give Hattie my new motivational playlist. It

the William Joseph piano piece to create the atmosphere.

I allow .... · one quick clip of *Wings are made to fly*, then move on to *Heroes* by David Bowie. The best part is my own beat-box creation with the following lyrics:

'Goal! Always believe in your boot.

You have the power to shoot.

You are unbeatable.

Always believe in you.

Score a Goal!'

And I finish with *We are the Champions*. It pays to be optimistic.

27: LAST TRAINING SESSION

This Friday is a teacher-training day so we'll be off school, which is handy as that's when Grandpa and I have to go to London for the filming of the show.

I'm trying to keep busy and not think too much about it; otherwise I come over all hot and sweaty.

Today, Thursday, we're having our last training session at school ahead of the football final on Saturday. The two most exciting events in my life are both happening in the space of a couple of days. It's crazy. Grandpa says it's like buses, you wait for ages for one to arrive and then two come at once.

As usual, the weather interferes. Due to the non-stop drizzle and the grounds man's desperate attempts to protect the pitch for Saturday's final, we're training in the sports hall.

"I think we need a shooting drill," says Coach.

"That's just for the strikers," moans Diego. "Boring."

Luckily Coach doesn't hear as he places cones around the hall. I wonder if he saw the practice I did on the field with Hattie after school the other day.

Al turns on Diego. "It's not just strikers who need to pass accurately." Tensions in the team are rising in the lead up to the big game.

"We all need to practice," Erica chips in. I suspect she's just saying it because she fancies Al. Most girls do.

I try to smooth things over. "Diego, think of it as a chipping drill or making *accurate* lay-offs. They need practising."

"You are absolutely right, Barney." Coach returns to the team, making me jump. "Chipping, passing, long ball, short ball: it's not just shots at goal that need to be accurate."

Diego stares at me. I can feel my cheeks burning up.

Coach points out the exercises spread around the room and explains the shots he wants us to practise. We could have done with more of this from the beginning of the season. In most of his lessons we just play a game. It's incredible that we've got so far in the competition. If it wasn't for a few terrific players I think we'd have struggled. People like Al, have carried us through the season…and Hattie, I guess.

There, I admit it. My sister is a good player. Better than me because I'm just average.

We make a start, shooting, laying off, passing.

'Happy Barry' blasts a ball so close to my legs, I have to jump out of the way.

"He nearly knocked you over!" laughs Al.

"Soz," Barry calls out.

"Yeah, he's got a strong boot when he kicks a stationary ball. Shame he's not as good when the ball's moving," I say to Al as I pass him. Al laughs. I walk on to the next exercise.

"Is this the chipping practice?" I ask Eddie.

"I didn't know there was one. I'm just copying Erica," he tells me.

Erica can boot the ball hard, but she can't chip. There's no hope for Eddie learning in that case.

On the next task, waiting in line, Lizzie is hula hooping.

"Hula hoop's for sissies," sneers Vijay.

"Just coz you can't do it," Lizzie snaps back.

Vijay ignores her, pulling himself up onto the mini climbing wall.

At the front of the queue, Hattie is talking under her breath. Frowning, she fires a shot at a cone, taking it out completely.

"What were you saying to yourself?" I ask as she passes me.

"School report," she murmurs. Her big meeting with Dad is scheduled after school today.

Now Cathy is trying to copy Lizzie, but she struggles to wriggle her short body in the right direction. Each time, the hoop starts on her waist and quickly spins down to her ankles.

"I've got an idea," I say to Cathy. She ignores me, picking up the hula-hoop and starting again.

I walk towards Coach, heart beating fast. "Sir."

"Yes, Barney." He doesn't look at me, too busy watching his favourite player strike the ball. Al fires it wide of the cone and halfway up the wall. "Your ankle's still weak. Don't put too much pressure on it, and we'll see how you go. Hopefully you'll be able to play the last ten minutes." Al's head drops, and he drags his feet along to the next drill.

Coach turns to me. "What is it?"

"I have an idea about the chipping and the shooting practice, sir." I sound like a squeaky mouse.

"Go on."

"I thought…"

"Vijay, get down!" Coach bellows, his voice echoing around the hall.

I take a deep breath and begin again. "I thought we could hang the hula hoops on the climbing wall at different heights. You can either chip or shoot into the hoops," I suggest.

"Anything to get that boy off that wall and those girls out of the hula hoop contest. Come on, help me set it up then." Coach strides off.

"At least someone's got some good ideas," Al grumbles.

With a small fist pump I follow Coach over to create my new invention.

28: CONSEQUENCES

At six o'clock, Hattie's summoned to Dad's office, 'The Shed', for the consequences discussion. Hattie will have a plan. Appealing to his weaker side, I expect.

I sneak after her down the garden in the dark and hide in a bush at the side of the shed.

Dad begins with his lecture on the importance of schoolwork and Hattie's poor attitude. In the glow of the shed light I watch a trail of ants climbing the branch next to me.

Hattie gets in early. "I have a dream." Her voice dances. I've heard that line somewhere. "I want to be a sporting phenomenon."

She stole those words from me!

"The build up to the football final is inspiring me so much. I feel that sport is taking over my life." What a drama queen. I peer through the leaves and in through the shed window.

"I forgot about how important my work should be." Her voice begins to wobble. "I don't have as many brains as Barney."

"Typical," I tut.

She sniffs loudly. "But I've been working so hard on sport, Dad." I peer in to see him handing her a tissue.

Dad buckles in less than thirty seconds. "Promise me you'll concentrate in class this term, Hattie, and improve these French results especially."

However, the wailing grows louder.

"Hey, Hattie, don't cry," Dad says softly.

"I thought…," sniff, "you'd be pleased," sniff, snort, sniff, "that I've been nominated for player of the season," she howls. How can girls produce that many tears?

"I am, I am," Dad looks like he's sweating. "In fact, I was thinking of offering you an incentive to do better in your exams."

Talk about gullible.

"Like a new pair of football boots?" Hattie says in a small voice.

I snort, splattering an ant with a blob of my snot. Wiping my nose on my sleeve, I stamp out of the bush and stomp back up the garden.

What about an incentive for me?

Hattie is clever, that's for sure.

***

I lie on my bed with my headphones on, trying to calm my brain. Morning and night, over and over, I can't stop running through all the possibilities of what might happen at the filming of the TV show. I've been losing sleep. On Monday I got in trouble for dozing off during the history lesson.

"Earth is over 150 million kilometres from the sun." I chant quietly. "Imagine you are over 150 million kilometres from the television cameras."

I hope this helps. Filming starts tomorrow. I'm running out of time.

29: UNDER SCRUTINY

"Barnaby Frank!" the producer bellows from the other end of the room.

I stand up ahead of Grandpa and walk over to shake the producer's hand like Grandpa said I should. A tall, square-shouldered man with hairy nostrils looks down at me. It's the kind of thing you notice when you're short.

"You're a kid!" he exclaims.

Well spotted.

"More of a small but knowledgeable person," I suggest. He bends down and eyeballs me. This is probably a test to see if big people scare me. Being able to see exactly how his contact lenses move around his eyeballs is distracting though.

"Professional football's a tough business, Barnaby. It's not for kids." I'm nearly choking on the garlic fumes spilling from his mouth.

"By Jove, you've got the wrong end of the stick, old boy," Grandpa calls out. He strides over to join me.

"Who are you?" asks the producer abruptly, searching the names on his clipboard.

"Barnaby Frank Senior," says Grandpa, standing to attention behind me. "Young Barney Junior here is my accomplice, acting as my second pair of eyes and ears. Get to my age, old fella, and it's good to have a back-up."

As Grandpa is talking, an elderly man, wearing a velvet waistcoat, walks in waving a steel-capped wooden stick. "Are we ready? I haven't got much time today," he roars across the room.

"Nothing wrong with being old now is there?" says Grandpa purposefully staring over the producer's shoulder towards the grand gentleman who's now being shown to a seat.

"You'd better have got me someone worth looking at today after the rubbish you made me sit through yesterday," grumbles the old man, squeezing his round body into the tub chair.

"That's Lord Loadsa, the Harlimac Chairman," I mutter.

"Cheryl!" The producer summons a smartly dressed young woman with a clipboard. She totters across the studio floor in a pair of very high heels. "Show these two to their places. Get another chair for the kid."

There are ten entrants in the filming today. Another group were seen yesterday, and apparently there are a further eight days of filming rounds. So, I figure that's about 100 contestants still in the competition.

We sit next to a pudgy man whose cheeks bulge out like a couple of red tomatoes. Shirtsleeves rolled up to his elbows, he leans forward against the table.

"Bill Costly, nice to meet ya," he says in a strong northern accent. "I'm the manager of the Local Lads under 15's, very successful." He offers Grandpa his hand.

"Barnaby Frank, nice to meet you." Grandpa shakes Bill's hand firmly.

"I see ya brought your little grandson with you." He winks at me. "Exciting, ain't it, laddie? You come along to watch the professionals in action?"

I copy Grandpa's lead, offering out my hand to shake and saying nothing but 'hello'. We sit down.

Bill leans towards us, cocking his head. "I've been checking out the competition," he confesses. "Nothing too much to worry about. Although you wanna keep an eye out for that shiny suit down there." He looks along the line of contestants. "Says he's from London, but he's got a strange accent, calls himself José, spells it with a J but sounds like Hosé. Bit shifty if you ask me. Gotta watch him. Know what I mean."

"Enlightening, thank you Bill," Grandpa replies. Bill tips his finger to his nose and sits back in his chair. The producer calls us all to attention.

"Right, everybody, I'm going to explain a few rules. This morning the panel will ask you questions in turn and then at random." He reads from his clipboard a list that he must have to repeat every day. "You can answer only when questioned."

"Err…" José, the man in the shiny suit, raises his hand.

The producer ignores him. "There is to be no interrupting. Everyone will be given an equal chance to display his or her knowledge." José raises his hand higher. "Your progress in the competition will be made known to you at a later date. The panel's decision is final." José's hand falls. "Right, lights on!" The producer slaps his clipboard down on the desk. Bright lights blind us. I turn away from the glare. "Let's begin by introducing your question panel."

A clapperboard snaps in front of the cameras, and filming begins. I try to breathe slowly but my heart is banging in my ears.

"One of the longest serving men at Harlimac Football Club," announces a voice from a loudspeaker, "Chairman Lord Loadsa!"

The contestants join in with the fake clapping being played in the background. It's so realistic, I even turn around to check no one's actually sitting there. Lord Loadsa stays firmly seated, waving to the audience (all eleven of us). It's quite possible that he's stuck in that chair.

"Next up, you don't want to upset this lady, because she pays the wages - Manageress Rachel Wise."

Somebody wolf whistles.

"Blimey, that's a mistake," Grandpa mutters, looking down the line.

I've heard of people having an aura and now I know what they mean. A woman walks on from the wings, dressed in a smart navy suit, her silky hair chopped just above her shoulders. Ms Wise glides into position, her dark eyes scanning the faces of the contestants. I shiver even in the heat of these dazzling lights.

"Finally, it's everybody's favourite footballing legend, your host Reggie Hunter!"

Reggie retired from professional football only last year to become a TV host. He swapped his Rovers shirt and shorts for a smart three-piece suit and shockingly bright tie. He dances onto the stage, dribbling a football, flicks it up in the air, bows to the camera and catches the ball on the back of his neck. The fake audience is going crazy, screaming and whistling. I jump out of my seat, clapping so hard it hurts my palms.

Grandpa tugs at my shirt. "Calm down, Barney. We've got to remain focused," he warns me.

"Hattie is never going to believe this," I croak. My tongue feels like sandpaper.

The questioning is about to begin. My stomach is somersaulting like a gymnast on the high bars.

"Action!"

Straight away Reggie points to Bill Costly, our neighbour. "What's your view on buying new players?"

"Buy, buy, buy!" bellows Bill. "You gotta spend to get the best. There's no way round it." He's smiling, clearly spoken. It even looks like he's enjoying the limelight. How can he act so confident under all this pressure? "Who's scored this season, eh? Three players, the rest of em, get rid of em. You gotta buy the top blokes. Expensive, but if they're good, it's worth splashing the cash. Top scorers, buy 'em!" He taps his nose and points towards Lord Loadsa.

Punchy but expensive I think. Maybe this nose tapping is a nervous twitch. Reggie fires the same question at José, whose suit sparkles in the light. Maybe I should've let Grandpa wear his gold outfit after all.

"I vill choose ze best, for sure, but I vill get a good price. I know people..."

"Incentivise them," I mumble to Grandpa whilst José is ranting on. "Don't change the players straight away, juggle them up and offer them a reason to perform. Then see who's worth keeping." I hate to admit it but Dad's new football boots scheme has got Hattie working already. She was beavering away on her French verbs when we left the house this morning.

'What with?' writes Grandpa discreetly on the notepad.

All I can think about is Dad offering Hattie incentives to do well at school. I'm having a blank moment. Oh help. I feel like I've been sucked into a bubble. I can see and hear what's going on around me but can't react.

"Barnaby Frank, what's your opinion?" asks Reggie, cutting José short.

A camera is wheeling closer to me. I feel the heat as a spotlight shines in my eyes. Grandpa nudges me. This is my first chance to shine and I've lost my voice. I fiddle with the top button of my blue shirt. My body is on fire. Under the table, Grandpa's foot taps against mine.

"Incentivise them," I squeak. There is a long pause. Reggie is staring at me, waiting for more. I try to concentrate on his terrible tie. It's so bright that the spots stick in my vision, floating around the room. 'Believe in yourself Barney', I remember Mum telling me. I take a large gulp of water. "Don't sack any of them straight away but make them work for their place." I say. I check out the panel for a reaction, but they offer no clues.

On the table, a hand pulls at my little finger directing it to Grandpa's doodles on the pad.

"It's a carrot!" I say out loud by mistake.

Chuckling, Lord Loadsa sits forward in his chair, resting his hands together on the table. "A carrot?" he laughs.

"Dangle a carrot in front of the donkey," pipes Grandpa. I take another gulp of water, thankfully I'm cooling down. Now I remember, one of Grandpa's favourite catchphrases.

"Take all their toys away." Grandpa leans forward, mirroring the Lord's actions. "The fast cars, the big salaries - and offer them back on a performance-or-win bonus basis."

One bushy eyebrow creeps further up Lord Loadsa's forehead. His fingers massage his lips as he chews on our idea. Leaning across to Reggie, he mutters into his ear. The contestants wait patiently, apart from José, who shuffles his swinging feet and snorts. Reggie starts writing on his notepad.

Was that one nil to us?

***

Question after question fires along the line. How can you improve defence? What do you think of players' fitness? How will you select players?

José mistakenly mentions the success of his fantasy football team, letting Rachel Wise pounce.

"All the other players in your league are registered to the same account. Do you have a lot of brothers and sisters José?" she queries.

Apparently immune to embarrassment, he shakes his dark mane.

"It must be difficult to lose if *you are* every team in the league," she hisses. "Still didn't manage to score very highly, though, did you?" Her words scratch his success to shreds.

José tips his sunglasses down from his forehead to his nose, slumping in his chair, long legs sprawling across the floor. "Pah," he shrugs.

"Whereas young Barnaby, not only came second in his fantasy league, he ranks in the top fifty nationally."

Once again, the eyes of the room turn my way. A camera zooms towards me. My jaw drops open, giving it a full view of my braces. Grandpa slaps me on the back. Ms Wise's eyes transfix me.

"What a shame you sold Vanson before the last game," she purrs.

How did she know that?

"Cut!" The producer interrupts to issue instructions. "Let's take five. Reggie get ready to start again with your demo."

"Catching flies again, mate," jokes Bill Costly nudging me with his elbow. "Big brother's watching you," he warns out of the corner of his mouth. I look across to see José sneering at the end of the row, the studio light glinting off his gold teeth.

I close my mouth. The show is already moving on.

30: COMPETITION PRESSURE

"Action!" The clapperboard snaps down.

Reggie Hunter loosens his tie, takes off his jacket and walks to centre stage. Clipboard Cheryl throws him a football, and he begins keepie-ups, back kicks and tricks for us all to marvel over.

"Footwork skills, your greatest friend or your worst enemy. I want drills to improve them. You've got five minutes."

Contestants begin scribbling on paper whilst Grandpa and I whisper ideas to one another. With the keepie-up drill ending in the smashed greenhouse disaster and the dribbling drill putting me off chocolate for life, I'm not hopeful about our chances on this one.

The seconds tick by.

"Time's up." Reggie points at our neighbour. "Bill Costly, let's hear from you first."

Bill stands up, pushing his shirtsleeves over his elbows.

"Football tennis!" he calls out. "If I might explain?" He waits for Reggie to nod. "The idea is to improve your control of the ball on first contact in the air. You mark out an area, like the size of a tennis court, with a long hip-height net dividing the two sides. The aim of the game is to kick the ball back across the net from player to player. If the ball hits the ground on your side of the net, you lose a point."

I can imagine playing that game at school - a good answer, in my opinion. Reggie signals for Bill to sit down.

Next up is the only lady in our group, a referee. However, all her suggestions are complicated. I'm totally confused by all the rules before she even starts describing the task. The panel spends a lot of time trying to clarify all the conditions, annoying some of the other contestants.

"Reggie, zat is favouritism, you're helping her," spits José as the lady is given another chance to simplify her idea. "You're letting her 'ave another turn. What about the rest of us, eh?"

Reggie glares at him, but addresses the issue. "I'm going to give you five minutes to simplify your idea whilst I ask one more contestant. Then we move on to another subject. Ok?" The ref lady mouths a thankyou.

"'Bout time, I 'aven't 'ad a go yet," José moans. Lord Loadsa looks warningly over his spectacles at the shiny suit.

"Because I think your idea has potential," Reggie adds. The ref lady's eyes widen. That's the first time they've encouraged anyone. "Fred Hooper, we haven't heard much from you."

José crashes back into his chair and crosses his arms, sulking.

Attention turns to the tall, slim man sitting next to José. He's the only contestant wearing a tie. Unclipping his briefcase, he slides out a pile of papers stapled in one corner. "May I?" He stands up and offers them to the panel.

Rachel beckons him forward. He steps around the table and approaches the bench. The papers flap about in his shaking hands.

"Can you explain these drawings?" Ms Wise asks with a smile.

Fred wriggles in his shoes, his heels rising up and down. I feel twitchy just watching.

"Well, I...," he peers at the first sheet, "er, not, not this page." The panel watches the pages being shuffled in front of them but Fred can't seem to find what he's looking for. "Sorry, I'll just..." He waves his thumb over his shoulder, turns and trots back to his briefcase, flipping open the lid. "I-uh, I took the wrong paper," he explains. "It's here somewhere," he apologises, his head hidden in the case. The panel glance at one another. Rachel taps her long manicured fingernails on the desk. Fred Hooper's pitch is falling apart.

Frantically, he searches through the sheets, pushing papers to the side of his case until a pile topples over the edge and sprays across the floor.

"Oh fiddle!" Fred flaps, swaying from one foot to another. Scraping his chair back, Reggie gets up to help retrieve the papers, but as he approaches Fred flings an arm out to stop him like a traffic policeman.

"No!" *Awkward.* "No, I don't mean to be rude, Mr Hunter." Fred's head drops, he looks at the mess on the floor. We are all watching and waiting.

"It's all been a big mistake!" he wails. "I quit."

Exit via door one!

"Cut!" shouts the producer. "Let's take an early lunch."

Grandpa collapses back into his chair. "Phew! We can breathe again."

31: LORD LOADSA

"That was rubbish, your first answer, Barney," says Bill Costly over lunch. He stuffs another prawn sandwich into his big mouth in one go, spitting bits out as he talks. "If you don't pay 'em, the players'll just walk away and go somewhere else."

His hand dives in on the last ham and cheese sandwich, which technically should be mine. I eat two sandwiches in the same time that Bill Costly demolishes five!

"Who's going to want to buy them if they're not winning?" I ask.

"There's so much money flying about. You're too young to understand." He shakes his head and plunges his yellow teeth into the bread. I wonder if they're false, like Grandpa's.

"I can't imagine a wise man would keep pumping money into a failing club for too long," says Grandpa.

"How are we all enjoying lunch?" Lord Loadsa walks up behind me. Automatically, most of the contestants sit to attention. This is the first time he's spoken to any of us. I wonder if he heard what Grandpa was saying.

"Great spread," pipes Bill. Everyone mumbles in agreement. "Lovely sandwiches," Bill continues. "I bet you're more used to Champagne and caviar, eh?" Bill winks at Lord Loadsa. I'm so glad Grandpa doesn't do that.

"So, Barnaby Junior, what's a young lad like you doing here helping out your Grandpa?" Lord Loadsa asks me, resting a hand on my shoulder. I look up at his white bearded face. He reminds me of Father Christmas, which makes me feel relaxed.

"Yeah, wouldn't you rather be at home playing with your train set?" cackles Bill. How does he know we have a train set?

Lord Loadsa cocks his head. "Do you have a train set, or is Mr Costly picking on you?"

Bill goes a bit pink.

I bounce on my seat. Ha! You're rumbled, Costly. "Actually," I announce to the table. "My Grandpa has an amazing train set and he lets me help out sometimes."

"Marvellous, what type?" The Lord turns his attention to Grandpa. "Got a Hornby Double O myself."

"The same," Grandpa replies.

"Flying Scotsman's my favourite of course, though I've just bought the London Olympic train. Hopefully it'll become a collector's item in the future."

Grandpa and Lord Loadsa get stuck into a discussion about scenery and track layouts. The ref lady goes back to her lunch, nibbling at a piece of cake and making the odd comment to her neighbour. José is busy typing on his phone, his chair turned away from the table and his straggly legs spread out into the path of the waiter who does well not to trip over them. The other contestants stare at the train enthusiasts chatting. I bet they wish they had a train set.

Bill Costly sits dribbling like a hungry wolf, his red cheeks blazing.

"Ah, the old milk lorry, I remember those as a kid," says Lord Loadsa.

"Mine's stuck in the middle of a pond." Grandpa begins to chuckle. "I was trying to do a water feature and the lorry rolled in whilst the liquid was setting!"

Hugging his ribs, Loadsa lets out a full belly laugh.

Cheryl with the clipboard appears. "Time to start filming again, Sir," she chirps. "If you'd like to take your positions."

Bill shoots up. "I'm ready to get back to business," he broadcasts.

"Nice talking to you, Barnaby and Barney. Good luck." Lord Loadsa shakes Grandpa's hand and then mine.

"Thank you, Sir," I reply, only just remembering my manners. He points his stick and marches away.

"My milk lorry's stuck in a pond!" I hear Bill mimic as we walk past.

Grandpa winks at me. "Ready for round two."

32: BILL COSTLY VERSUS ME

The atmosphere is so electric that even the hairs on my arms are standing up. Reggie fires questions, triggering instant answers from contestants. Everyone leans forward in their seats, except José who's slouching, with his legs sprawling across the floor. My eyes are wide open, watching, waiting. I'm ready.

"What coaching experience do you have, Barnaby Frank?"

"We've been coaching the Harlimac Harrier to be a sporting phenomenon." I start listing all the drills I've put Hattie through. The panel appears to be interested. "The team that she plays for is in the County Football Championships Final this year. And she's been nominated for the 'Player of the Season' award." It's important to end on a positive note. I don't mention that it's a school competition.

Ms Wise turns her attention to our neighbour, scanning him with a critical eye. Bill starts to shuffle in his seat. Suddenly, she points her silver fountain pen at him. "Bill Costly, you coach a youth team. How well have they done this season?"

Bill flinches. "We've been plagued by injuries, plagued." He shakes his head.

"Are you saying that you haven't had a good season?" Rachel Wise interrupts, like a judge in a trial. "Because I've done a little research of my own. Contrary to the information on your application form, I understand that your team was promoted last season, and although you started well this year, it looks like you'll be lucky to avoid relegation."

That's one thing he's got in common with Harlimac!

Beads of sweat are oozing out of Bill's shiny forehead. "Unfortunately two of our best strikers moved out of the area." Bill pulls a white handkerchief from his pocket and mops his brow. He continues. "And the goalie, well, that kid's got issues, but it's not my place to say. I'm on the lookout for a replacement."

He must have come up with some amazing ideas to get on the show if his current team is that bad.

"We'll be back fighting next year, you mark my words," he assures the panel.

Ms Wise stares at him without smiling.

I gulp down a second glassful of water and fan my face with paper. I'm glad I didn't wear a jumper. Thankfully the producer announces a pause in the filming whilst they adjust the lighting and touch up Reggie's and Rachel's make-up.

"The barrage of questions is endless," comments Grandpa.

"Yeah, my brain's fizzing," I reply.

Aware of the grilling Bill Costly just suffered from the Manageress, I try to keep my focus whilst she's being groomed.

"She's meant to be the scariest woman in football," I say to Grandpa, covering my lips with my hand.

Uh-oh, I grit my teeth as her glare lands on my face. I worry that the compliment she gave me earlier is already forgotten.

"Cameras roll," calls the producer. "Action."

Cue Rachel Wise… "We're interested to know what other areas of the club you believe need changing, be it our spending or costs. Not necessarily player related; it could be facilities, advertising, promotions..." She points her pen in our direction.

"That's like I said at the beginning," Bill mutters, his tomato cheeks bulging in a cheesy smile.

Said what?

Ms Wise's eyes narrow to slits. It's difficult to tell if they are even open at all beneath those long black lashes. She interrupts Bill.

"Actually I wanted to hear from Barnaby Frank Junior." Bill stops talking and sinks back into his chair, scratching his head. The Manageress continues. "Or shall I call you Barney." It wasn't a question because she didn't give me a chance to reply. "What are your views?" *Answer me boy!* she might as well have added.

Words come spewing out of my mouth. "Look at the cost of the club kit. I know it earns the club money but it all costs so much as well as the tickets."

Rachel's face softens, and her lips curl as if she's going to smile. I think she likes me. This is my chance to go for it whilst she's on my side.

All the playground gripes start coming out. "Some boys in my class are lucky enough to get a new kit every Christmas, but most of us have to make do with the same kit year on year. My mate Hugh's been told to stop growing by his mum because she can't afford to buy him any more kit." Reggie and some of the other contestants laugh. I don't think 'Hogger Hugh' finds it funny. "If the kit cost less then wouldn't more people buy shirts?"

Lord Loadsa nods.

I carry on. "And since you've sold half the team this season, people have got shirts with players' names on their backs that don't even play for the club any more!"

A finger taps my hand on the desk. Beside me Grandpa does a little cough.

"Couldn't you make the names attach by zip or Velcro so you can change them? Some of us have more than one favourite player."

Grandpa whistles but Reggie grins.

"Good idea. What about a birthday special - if it's your birthday everyone buys your name to stick on their shirt for the day." His sparkly white teeth twinkle in the lights. I wonder if he's ever been asked to do toothpaste adverts. He waves his hand in an arch. "Twenty thousand fans, all with Reggie Hunter written on their backs. I like it, I like it a lot."

"An interesting angle," Ms Wise comments whilst watching Reggie's display. "Very amusing."

I join in. "Players' names, autographs, faces, the possibilities are endless." This is fun.

Reggie sits down, scribbling on his pad. Grandpa is tugging at my shirt but I'm on a roll. "How about family tickets in the cheap seats up on the top tier? At least it would help fill the ground and make a better atmosphere. And a good atmosphere will spur the team on."

Reggie is still writing, Lord Loadsa is covering his mouth with his hand, but his jigging body makes me think he's chuckling. Ms Wise sits backs in her chair, interlocking her fingers. She bows her head. I guess this is my cue to be quiet now too.

"What are your views, Mr Costly?" she asks without looking up. With elbows resting on the table, she smoothes her eyebrows with her fingers. Maybe I went too far.

"It's an income source, ain't it?" pipes Bill, not bothered by the earlier criticisms. "You gotta keep putting the price up slowly month on month so that no one notices. If a fan changes their mind about their favourite player or that player leaves then it's more pennies in the bank for the club because they'll wanna buy another shirt. You and I are business people, Rachel. We understand these things." He glances in my direction.

Bill just called the Manageress, Rachel! You can't do that without asking permission. It's like calling the Queen 'Liz'!

She glances up, her features expressionless.

"Keep 'em spending," Bill ends with a wink and his customary tap of the nose.

"It's a shame you didn't come up with any of your own ideas, Mr Costly, rather than criticising and reinventing someone else's work." Looking down at the desk Ms Wise makes what appears to be a big cross on her pad.

Bill stands up to protest.

"That's all for now, thank you."

Stand down from the dock, Bill Costly, you're finished!

33: THE ACADEMY KID

"I'd like to introduce our young academy player, Maxime Buti."
Reggie invites a wavy-haired guy dressed in full Harlimac kit onto
the stage.

I'm grinning so wide it hurts.

As he jogs onto the stage, Reggie continues. "This twenty-one
year old Frenchman made his debut against Chelsea just a few
weeks ago. A player to watch out for in the future."

Buti waves to the contestants. For a minute I forget where I am
and nearly jump up to ask for his autograph.

"Your next task is to devise a training session aimed at
strengthening a particular skill of your choice. In a separate studio,
we have set up a mini football pitch with a full sized goal and as
many balls as you need. You can make any reasonable request for
extra pieces of equipment if necessary." Reggie puts his hand on
Buti's shoulder. "So in twenty minutes, you will be training this man."
He pats the player on the back.

Hattie's gonna be so jealous.

"We're coaching a Premiership player," I giggle. My insides are
churning.

"An academy player," Grandpa reminds me.

"He's played against Chelsea."

"He came on for the last twenty minutes do you remember?" he asks me.

"Er, yeah, I think so." I don't.

"Hmm, didn't stand out but the kid shows promise."

"Yeah," I agree. I wonder if I am *showing promise*.

I can't stop wriggling. Maxime Buti and the panel are walking into the training room along with the producer and most of the cameramen. Cheryl with the clipboard is wandering along the line of contestants.

"I think I need the loo. We're not being filmed now are we?" I ask Grandpa.

"Go on then but be quick because we've got to have an idea of what we're doing when you get back."

I check with Cheryl before dashing off to the bathrooms. I'm desperate. It must be all the water I've been guzzling down.

"I'll happily go first," Bill Costly says to Cheryl as I'm walking back across the studio on my return. "I just need six cones."

She notes the request down on her clipboard.

I slip into my seat.

Bill leans towards Grandpa and hisses "they always remember the first one." He picks at his teeth with his tongue. "I'm gonna take a leak before I'm called."

"When do we go?" I ask quietly as Bill strides out. "Second, so we need to get a move on."

I begin scribbling pictures of the various tasks I'd set Hattie, so that Grandpa and I can decide which one to use. We're in agreement almost immediately.

Bill's barrel-like figure rolls back into the room just as his name is called. He waves at Cheryl, spinning on his heels and heading in her direction. "Let's see how good this boy really is, shall we?" he jokes to the rest of us.

Are people laughing at him or with him? Hard to tell.

Bill disappears through a doorway in the far corner of the studio. The door clicks shut behind him, leaving the rest of us to wait and think about our ideas.

"So this is going to be my job," Grandpa points to my diagram.

"Yes, I'll take care of this section here," I tell him, not actually feeling as confident as I may seem. I know that my idea works with Hattie, and the target practice is definitely helping with the school team too. I've just never put the combination together like this before.

Cheryl returns with her clipboard and sits at one of the seats on the panel. I start to label up sheets of paper in big writing from one to eight.

"Shall we ask for the materials then?" Grandpa suggests.

I raise my hand. We have two requests. "Please may we have a ball of string and some scissors?"

She notes it down.

"And some Blu-Tac."

She adds it to her list, tears off the page and hands it to one of the technicians.

On the other side of the room, José whips out his phone and starts tapping away. He doesn't even put the phone on silent, so the noise rattles around the studio.

Cheryl's beady eyes survey the line of contestants. Spying the culprit, she rises, and her red patent shoes snap across the hard floor. She halts in front of José, who looks up.

Cheryl points at the phone with her pen and shakes her head. "I think you're aware of the no phone rule," she spits out of lips painted to match her shoes.

José holds up his hands. "But I just need to make a quick call," he whines.

"No phones at any point," she states.

Shiny suit turns the phone off and slips it into his pocket, bottom lip stuck out like a sulky kid.

"Nah, nah, nah. I said take it right. You're going left!" Bill Costly's voice booms from behind the closed doors.

The player shouts something back, but we can't hear what.

"Your left but my right," bellows Bill. "Try again. Last time."

I begin a giggle that ripples through Grandpa and passes on to the smiling ref lady.

I punch a hole in the top of each sheet of paper to thread the string through. We're up next.

34: BOSSING BUTI

My idea is to split the goal into a grid of eight squares by tying string to the cross bar and posts. Using my hole-punched papers, we number the squares, starting at 1 in the bottom left hand corner and ending with 8 in the top right. We use the Blu-Tac to stop the string moving around the posts and to weigh down each vertical string. If only Grandpa's 'shunter' projection was more developed and we could just project a grid onto the front of the goal.

"Remember we can only do our best," says Grandpa before we begin.

"Our best just has to be amazing," I reply. I try to stand up as straight as possible.

Maxime Buti stands in front of me, his wavy hair tied back by a band across his forehead. He is much bigger than me but only just taller than Grandpa, probably because he has more hair. Thankfully, keeping busy setting up the task with the string has kept my mind off the fact that I'm about to tell a Premiership player what to do.

I put my hand out as Reggie Hunter introduces us. "Bonjour." I try out my best French accent. "Je m'appelle Barney." I tell him. It means, 'my name is Barney.'

Buti shakes my hand. It's the first time I realise that he has only two fingers and a thumb on his right hand. "Bonjour," he replies.

I try not to stare at his hand. He plays football with his feet, why am I concerned about his hand? Concentrate on your French greetings Barney.

"*Ca va?*" I ask - 'how are you?'

"*Oui, ca va bien merci.*" He replies - 'yes, very well thank you'.

I don't know how anyone else is reacting to our conversation because I am so focused on the task. Buti's smiling. I think he's impressed I'm making an effort.

"Barnaby will throw the ball into play somewhere inside the box." I point to Grandpa and then the box. "You must collect the ball and shoot at the numbered square that I call out." I look Maxime Buti straight in the eyes. They are bright blue.

"Ok," he says.

The first 'easy' ball is thrown in. Buti steps towards the slow rolling ball.

"One!" I shout.

Buti taps it into the bottom left-hand corner.

"Well done." I give him the thumbs up.

He jogs back and Grandpa throws in the next ball.

"Four!"

The striker chips the ball up into square number five, at the wrong end of the goal. What happened there? Buti smiles as he returns, so I smile back, hoping he'll get it right this time.

The ball flies in, and the player has to sprint.

"Five!" I cry. I figure that might be where he finds it easiest to shoot. He boots it hard, hitting the string between three and four on the lower level. Grandpa is grimacing. I have a cold, sinking feeling.

"No good?" Buti asks.

Absolute rubbish! But I can't tell him that. He played Chelsea a few weeks ago and he could be signed by Man United in the future for all I know.

"Um, well, I think we'll just go over it again." I pass him as he walks back to his place outside the box. Standing in front of the goal I point to the first square. "One!" I call out, moving along. "Two!" I can see Buti repeating my words under his breath. "Three!" he mouths after me. "Four!" I reach the last square on the lower level and walk back across the goal to point up to the top left. "Five!"

Buti bares his teeth and points at the top square. "Five?" he asks.

"Yes five," I reply.

"What is this square?" The footballer signals down to the bottom corner.

I walk back over to the square and say "four." He winces. "*Quatre*," I repeat in French.

"Ah, *quatre*. And this in French?" He walks over, directing me back to number five.

"*Cinq*."

"*Cinq*," he murmurs.

Why didn't I realise before that the numbers were confusing him?

"I can say them in French," I offer, pointing at one. "*Un, deux*," I move along the line and read out the rest in French too.

"Yes, yes," the Frenchman is nodding. "Is good, thank you." He jogs back outside the box.

I wave to Grandpa, who throws in the next ball.

"*Quatre!*" I call out, holding up four fingers. Buti slots the ball into the bottom right. He jogs past me. We start again.

"Six!" I figure that's a cross between French and English anyway. He hurls a ball up into box number six, just clipping the string. We carry on and his score rises to seven out of ten shots on target with three very near misses.

After the ten shots, Grandpa stops throwing. Either he needs a rest or he is ready to finish the session. Using my peripheral vision (I've been practising) I can see that Reggie and Lord Loadsa are in hot debate. The ex-professional is gesturing to the producer for us to wind up but Lord Loadsa is waving his finger as if objecting.

Our time is running out. We need to really show an improvement.

"Mr Buti!" I call. "Very good. *Tres bien!*" I give him the thumbs up and beckon him over.

"Please call me Maxime," he says in his French accent. I'm on first-name terms with a professional footballer! I try to keep cool, reminding myself that he's just another human being, even if he does have magical footballing powers and probably drives a Ferrari.

Slowly, I ask him to imagine, (tapping my head), a burning ball of fire in his body. "*Un feu dans le corps,*" I say in my best French accent. It's lucky I've just revised parts of the body for a French test at school next week. "Push the fire down your leg, '*la jambe*' and out through your foot, '*le pied*'. Kick the ball at the number 8, '*huit*', to win the World Cup."

"The World Cup," he whistles. I guess 'win the World Cup' is universally understood.

I twist my hands on top of one another like I'm holding a trophy and wave it above my head triumphantly. "OK?"

"*Oui, oui*, I understand now, *'huit'* is eight," says Maxime, cupping a fist in the other hand.

"Fire, body, leg, foot," I chant, slapping the appropriate part of my body. 'Eight, World Cup, boom!" And again: "Fire, body, leg, foot, eight, World Cup, boom!"

Maxime stamps his feet in time with my chanting.

"Fire, body, leg, foot, eight, World Cup, boom!" I get faster. "Fire, body, leg, foot, eight, World Cup, boom!" The footballer is stamping furiously.

I signal to Grandpa to throw the ball.

"Fire, body, leg, foot, eight, World Cup, boom!"

Maxime takes off across the box. I can almost see the flames in his legs.

"Fire, body, leg, foot, eight, World Cup, boom!"

He lunges and strikes. The ball flies across the goal face towards the top right-hand corner and straight into the middle of the number 8 box. The string doesn't even move.

Everyone jumps out of their seats and cheers - a standing ovation from Lord Loadsa, Reggie Hunter and Rachel Wise!

My eyes begin to swell with tears and I quickly wipe them away on my sleeve. They're happy tears but I still don't want anyone to see. Grandpa is pumping his fists.

The Frenchman runs back, does a celebratory dance and then high fives me.

"I feel like *I've* won the World Cup!" My voice is shaking.

Buti grabs my hand and pulls it up into the air. "Today, you are the champion!"

35: WHAT NOW?

Reggie scribbles notes as Rachel Wise dictates, and the producer ushers us out of the door. I take one last look back at Maxime Buti as we leave. He is drinking from a water bottle and doesn't see me, but Lord Loadsa looks across and salutes. I salute him in return.

The producer summons the next entrant, José, in his shiny suit. Grandpa and I float back to our seats.

"Actually," José whines as he walks towards the producer who is standing in the doorway. "Zee Barneys stole my idea. But I guess I'll just 'ave to come up with zumzing else."

"He must be joking!"

"Ignore him," Grandpa advises me. "He's just saying it to wind us up, and he probably hasn't got any ideas of his own."

"I told ya to watch him," says Bill, flicking his head in the direction of José's disappearing figure. "What did ya do in there?" he turns to look at us, holding a roll of chins in his stubby fingers. "Bit of role-play, get 'em cheering, eh?"

"Not exactly…"

"Good try, lad." Bill cuts me off, slapping me on the shoulder. He starts collecting his belongings. "I'm heading back up north to work on the next task. Bet you're hoping your Grandpa gets as far as I do, eh?"

So he isn't actually interested in how we got everyone cheering. He just wants to gloat about being the first to be going through. I stand with my hands on my hips. The man is rude and I might just tell him so.

"Good luck, Bill." Grandpa crosses his legs and pats my seat, giving me a 'sit down' look.

"Bye all, nice to meet ya. The next round beckons." Without waiting for responses, he waves and trots out of the studio.

"Doesn't he really annoy you, Grandpa?" My hands are still glued to my hips.

"I let it all waft over me," says Grandpa. He brushes his hand up over his head. "See, it's gone. I'm feeling very happy and I don't want some fool's words to spoil that."

I try brushing Bill's words over my head but I think they've got knotted up in my hair.

***

"I've just told a Premiership player what to do!" I squeal. "No one in the school team has ever met a Harlimac player in the flesh. Not even Vijay, and he's posh. His dad's been in a director's box."

"You'll be the envy of the playground." Grandpa looks around the empty carriage. A few more passengers are filing in at the other end. "Remember to keep your voice down. We're not supposed to talk about what went on."

"I know." I screw my nose up. "But I can't wait to tell Hattie, she'll be dead jealous."

127

"That she will, but you'll have to keep quiet for a while yet."

Invent a training machine. You have seven days to email your designs.

That's how we left the mysterious world of television, with those words ringing in our ears. Have we done well enough in the preliminary round? I think so. They seem interested, but how do you know what they are really thinking?

"Nobody said don't bother coming back!" I remind Grandpa as our train slides out of the station.

"Well that's positive, Barney!"

"I'm glad you and I are in this together, Grandpa." I slip my arm through his and rest my head against his shoulder.

"So am I, wouldn't miss it for the world."

"I think I'd burst if I couldn't talk about it to anyone."

"Now all we have to do is invent the most amazing training machine." Grandpa says in a hushed voice. "Any ideas?"

Minor problem. Number of ideas - zero!

36: TACTICS

"So, where have you been all day?" asks Hattie as I set up the chessboard with a tactical moves game I've invented. This should help us for tomorrow's final.

On our train journey home, Grandpa and I decided how we'd answer questions like this one. "I went to London with Grandpa. He wanted to show me all this war stuff at a museum."

"Why wasn't I invited?"

"Because you were already going to Olive's house, and you're not interested in the war."

"Nah! Glad I went to Olive's instead. We played with this really cool dance-mat game she's got. Olive got in a mood coz I'm better than her and she's been practising loads."

"Uh huh," I murmur. Sounds boring as anything. "So, you've got to imagine that the chess board is a football field. My rook is taking a throw in from the side line." I hold up the chess piece. "My king and queen are attacking the goal whilst the pawns are all defending." I point them out, standing in a straight line across the field from the rook.

"Yeah, OK."

"Imagine the queen moves several squares forward." I slide the queen down the board. "This draws the defending pawn away from the rook."

Hattie watches as I tap a pawn across three squares to follow the queen. Then I draw her attention to the king, all by himself on the opposite side of the board. Her eyes follow my finger.

"This opens up a clear line for the rook to throw to the king." I slide my forefinger between the two pieces. "So, in the final tomorrow, think about drawing players away to make openings."

Hattie is staring at the chess pieces, drumming the tips of her fingers against her lips. "But pawns can only move one space at a time," she says.

I am beginning to realise that my coaching success may depend on the imagination of my team.

I ask Hattie why she wants to win tomorrow's football final.

"Because I always want to win. I hate losing."

She's definitely got a killer instinct. She proves it by grabbing me in a headlock. Even though I can barely breathe, I refuse to give in. I never win against Hattie. Dad walks in.

"Supper's ready."

Hattie releases me, and a rare victory is mine.

"Lucky I saved you there, Barney," says Dad nudging me as I walk past. Trust him to spoil my winning mood.

***

"Grandpa told me that filming went very well today," Mum whispers as I get into bed, "and you met some famous footballers."

"He's supposed to have kept it a secret."

"I promise not to tell anyone." Mum kisses me goodnight. "Well done superstar."

I wrap my arms around her shoulders and squeeze tight.

37: OBJECTIVES

I'm in delayed shock. Yesterday was the most amazing, unbelievable, secret day of my life. Sadly this doesn't mean that I'm flooded with ideas for a training machine. More like I'm suffering from a drought.

But I can't even think about it since today is cup final day. Now is the time for last-minute coaching.

"Write down your objectives for the match," I tell my client.

"Objectives?" a big word that's lost on Hattie.

"What you aim to achieve." I leave her messy bedroom, carefully avoiding all her clothes and clutter littering the floor. It's like an obstacle course.

I return fifteen minutes later. She's written:

1. *Run fast.*

2. *Use Cathy on the wing, she's fast…sometimes.*

3. *Keep control when dribbling.*

I am nodding - these are all quite encouraging - until…

"*Shout at the defenders, Eddie and Diego*?" I read aloud.

"They don't do anything otherwise." Hattie's voice is sharp.

"That's not strictly an objective," I point out. "It's supposed to be positive."

She shrugs. I wait, hoping she'll think of two very important objectives. How can she miss these off the list?

When the silence lengthens and my ears start to burn, I suggest, "are you going to make any tackles?"

"Of course I am." Hattie slumps back in her chair and folds her arms. "It's going to be a tough match, Barney. They're last year's champions." She grabs a cushion and hugs it so tight the stuffing's liable to spill out.

"You've forgotten one very important thing." We're in trouble if she doesn't get this one.

Throwing the cushion aside, Hattie jumps up, grabs my shoulders, spins me round and shoves me towards the door. I hobble over a knot of beads, and try to shake off the fluffy hairband that's attached itself to my sock.

"Goodbye, Coach, I'm pre-match relaxing!" She pushes me out onto the landing and shuts the door behind me.

"What about scoring some goals?" I holler through the keyhole.

I put my ear to the door. 'Under Pressure' blasts from Hattie's iPad. It's her favourite 'Happy Feet' movie clip.

Let's hope her teammates are planning on scoring.

38: PRE MATCH

Hattie twitches all through lunch. When her legs stop jigging, her fingers start tapping. It's putting me off my chicken sandwich. I'm about to say something when Grandpa looks at me over the top of his glasses and shakes his head. I think it's worth wearing glasses just to perfect that disapproving look. I zip my lips.

After Hattie's third trip to the loo, we're finally getting in the car.

Grandpa puts a bobbly veined hand on her shoulders. "Don't worry," he says. "The minute that whistle blows, you'll be off like a rocket. You'll forget about those nerves. Barney's trained you well." At least someone recognises my efforts. "You'll be the one scoring goals and making tackles."

I slide across the back seats of the car, Hattie climbs into the middle and Grandpa lowers himself in on the far side.

I take a sly peek at her as we drive along. Head up, staring out of the windscreen, my sister sits biting her nails. This final is the highlight of her season. Apparently a selector from the county team will be watching. Even looking at Hattie in the wrong way today could make her burst into tears.

Dad hasn't noticed. "Have you practised your shooting this week, Hattie?" he asks, meeting her eye in the rear-view mirror. She nods.

"How about your tackles? You've got to make those tackles."

I've already made this point earlier. This isn't the time to be applying more pressure.

"Yes."

"Headers?" He looks up again into the mirror.

"Will you just concentrate on your driving!" squawks Mum.

"I'm just checking," he snaps.

He doesn't ask me anything. I may be on the bench but I'm still on the team and in the car.

***

We pull up into the car park at the playing fields. I take a good look around at the gathering crowd: mums, dads, uncles, aunties, granddads and handbag-wielding grannies. I wonder if there is any way that you can spot football scouts.

"Right, chaps." Grandpa releases his seatbelt and turns to face us both. "Remember, never stop playing until the whistle blows, but don't argue with the ref! Referees are like your parents: never mind if you think they've got it wrong, they are *always* right."

I'm not so sure about that, Grandpa.

"Onward soldiers!" he booms, clenching his fist in the air.

"Onward!" we chorus.

I'm ready, even if I am only on the bench.

"Mum, can I borrow your phone to make a match report and movie?"

"A movie? I don't think my phone has that sort of camera on it, Barney." She kisses me on the forehead. "Good luck." She waves as she walks off down the sideline. Sometimes technology is wasted on adults.

39: CUP FINAL

"This is a disaster," grumbles Grandpa as he watches beside me, hands in pockets, chin to his chest.

I stand up off the bench to talk to him. It's approaching half time, I haven't been on the pitch, and the team is losing two nil.

"Problems as I see them," I begin, "are in defence. Eddie and Lizzie are only any use if someone actually runs directly into them. Diego's trying his best - he's only tackled his own players twice so far. Olive's doing all right I suppose." She's actually really good but I'm not going to admit it in public. She is my replacement. "Midfield, we have a major issue." I watch Vijay back away from another tackle and then shout at Erica for not chasing after the player.

"Yeah, you're right," agrees 'Happy Barry', sat on the other end of the bench. I thought he was chatting to Al.

"It's no surprise that Erica's run out of puff," I carry on. "Cathy's frazzled; she's worked so hard covering for Angus, who still has no idea what game he's playing and hasn't dropped back past the half-way line at all."

"Is Angus, the boy with his socks around his ankles, Al's replacement?" asks Grandpa.

"Yeah. Al can't play for long because of his injury. Angus is nowhere near as good."

"At least the goalkeeper is doing well."

I squash Grandpa's positive remark, "until he forgot how to catch."

Barry roars with laughter.

"The coach has got his work cut out to come back from this," says Grandpa.

Coach is standing further down the pitch, screaming at the players. "Why isn't anyone shooting?"

Grandpa peers down the sideline at him.

I glance back at Al and Barry on the bench.

"Didn't do enough of your target practice, Barney," pipes Al as he watches the last few minutes of the half.

"Wish we'd done more sessions like that this season," says Barry.

"Yeah, you could've practised hitting a moving ball coz, like Barney says, you're a great shot when the ball is still," Al laughs. Barry elbows him.

"What sort of pass is that?" yells Coach, his face purple.

"He's doing it all wrong," I say quietly into Grandpa's ear.

"What? Speak up, I can't hear you."

"He's too negative," I say. Now Al and Barry are listening. "He's just telling them off for their mistakes." I turn away from the bench and whisper to Grandpa again. "It's what Dad did to Hattie for days after her report, focusing on how badly she'd done."

"You mean she only started working on her studies when he started praising her for what she was good at."

"Exactly! The incentives helped too." After her Oscar winning performance in the shed, I'm tempted to add.

"What do you think he should be doing?" Al stands up next to me.

You can do this, Barney. The best player is asking for your opinion. I have successfully trained a Premiership footballer. Surely I must know enough to help out our school team

"Encourage them to believe that they can make a comeback!" I say. "In 2005, Liverpool came back from three nil down at half time to win the UEFA Champions league final." Al nods, he knows the game I'm talking about - it's footballing history. I carry on. "In an interview, a Chelsea player once said that when he stood in the tunnel before the game, he just had to look around at his teammates to know that they could go out and win. They stepped onto the pitch *believing*."

Al's face goes blank. "We're not Chelsea."

"But we're not playing Man United or Arsenal. We're playing another bunch of twelve year olds that we can beat."

"Hear, hear, Barney. You should go and speak to the team," Grandpa suggests.

"Coach just tells us the same thing over and over again."

"And why do you think he does that?" There's a smile on Grandpa's face.

"Because we don't listen," I answer.

"Or think we know better," says Al. At least he's recognising his own faults.

"I just forget," Barry admits. "My mum says her words go in one ear and out the other."

"Would it annoy you if somebody didn't listen to you?" Grandpa asks all three of us.

"Yeah, it's rude not to listen," says Al.

"You might learn something," I add. This is a revelation for Barry.

"So really try to listen to what he says, and if you still think he's missing something, then make a suggestion," Grandpa advises us, whilst keeping one eye on the game.

We all take a deep breath in as Pighfield shoot. The shot is wide, and we can all breathe again.

"I can't tell the coach what to do! Why would he care what I have to say?"

Grandpa turns to me and raises his eyebrows. "Did I say that you should tell him?"

"No," pipes Al. "You said make a suggestion."

Grandpa smiles and nods gratefully at Al.

"You didn't listen." Barry prods my arm. "I heard that." He taps his head with his forefinger. "Logged it in here."

The whistle blows for half time.

"Now's your chance," says Al, standing up from the bench.

"That's a great idea. You'll be much more fun to listen to than Coach," says Barry. "I'll run ahead and warn the team." He sprints off.

I look around at the spectators, including Mum and Dad, who are wandering off to the vending van in search of hot drinks. I then look at the team, walking towards the goalmouth, their heads hanging.

"Choose your words carefully Barney and you can make a

difference." Grandpa clutches my shoulders and gives me a gentle push off the bench.

"But I..." I dig my heels in.

Dread grabs hold of my stomach and shakes it. My hands claw at my cheeks. What if my instincts about the game are wrong?

40: TEAM TALK

"We need you, Barney." Al grabs my arm. "The team needs you. Come on." He pulls me onto the pitch.

"I'm not...I'm not sure...," I stutter as Al drags me closer to the team.

"Guys we can do this," I hear Barry saying. "And Barney's going to tell us how."

"To have any chance of winning this game, you've got to listen to Barney, after Coach has spoken," Al adds as we arrive, panting.

Everybody listens when Al speaks. Even Hattie pays attention. Eleven sad faces look up at me and at Barry's big beaming grin. I lean against the goalpost for support. Their heads turn towards the coach as he stomps over to the goalmouth. The hand rubbing his forehead covers his eyes.

"Well we're in a right mess," he says, dragging his fingers down the sides of his face. "You're gonna have to play much better in the second half to have any chance." He rests his hands on his hips and sighs. "What's happened to your tackling? Where are your passes?"

Nearly everyone bows their head, not daring to draw attention to themselves whilst Coach moans on and on... Eddie is delving for earwax with his finger, so is unlikely to be listening anyway. Lizzie is re-plaiting her hair. "We didn't defend well...can't seem to shoot straight…," I am listening but he's still moaning. Even Barry's grin slides into a grimace.

"Right, that's all from me," he grumbles, having uttered not a single word of encouragement. "Does anyone else have anything to add?"

All is quiet. Al lifts his head and glares at me, his eyebrows shooting up under his fringe. He nudges Barry and nods his head towards me. Barry looks at Al, then at me, then back to Al who nods in my direction again. "Barney's got some great ideas!" spouts Barry like he's just remembered.

Suddenly everyone pays attention because they've been primed.

"Yeah they're really good," adds Al. Coach turns to me, his beady eyes pin me down.

"Well come on then lad, let's hear what you have to say."

I swallow, trying to wet my dry mouth. This is it, my time to go for it. I step over to the middle of the goalmouth and dive into my analysis. "The pressure is all on the opposition to defend. Think about it, they're frightened of losing their lead. But you, you've got nothing to lose!"

All eyes are on me. Erica's stare burns into my chest. Eddie's fishing for bogies. Thankfully I can't see Coach's face.

"We're going on the attack. If Cathy moves further up field with Hugh, they can draw their markers out to the wing to help open up space in the middle for Hattie to work." Cathy drums her feet on the ground and claps her hands. "Hattie, you drop back a little to win those midfield balls, release up the side for Hugh and Cathy, then sprint into the space they clear down the centre line." I pause to

---

143

check with the coach, but he remains motionless with a vacant gaze.

"I've got it. Just like the chess," says Hattie. So she *was* listening.

"Carry on lad," Coach signals. "You haven't got much time."

"Angus, Vijay, you're going to be working like a set of scales. We did it in practice last week. If one moves up to tackle and pass, the other drops back." I raise one hand and lower the other to demonstrate.

"That's not my job." I knew Vijay would be trouble.

"Your job is to keep the balance," Coach interrupts.

"It's a very important role," I add. Vijay's chin lifts.

"You need to help Angus, because he's not used to playing in Al's position," Coach chips in again. Vijay looks at Angus, flaring his nostrils. I hope he'll take up the challenge.

"Work together with short, quick passes," I say to the rest of the team. "Don't wait for the ball to come to you, go and get it. Keep them guessing before you break."

"Erica." She wipes a hand across her lips as I look at her. "I know you're tired but you've got to hold on for another twenty minutes. Play further back. Use that strong boot of yours, like Lizzie. You two should pair up like scales, too."

She puts her arm around Lizzie's shoulders.

"What about us?" asks the mouth that's just swallowed a bogie.

"Eddie and Diego, let's have some talking between the two of you. Keep checking where the other is. Call out, 'I'm going left, cover me'," and stay awake, I think.

Finally, I swing my gaze around to Olive, the new girl with the red wavy hair. She's waiting patiently, crouching on the pitch.

For some reason my voice croaks when I speak to her. "Olive." I cough to clear my throat. You've no idea how hard this is. "You're a really good defender. We need you as the last defence." She smiles at me.

The ref's whistle screeches behind me. The players start getting up. I stand square with my replacement.

"Stay solid for the first fifteen minutes, Olive, then when Barry comes on, you go right up front and score some goals."

"Yes!" Olive claps. Hattie joins in.

"Flying footballs!" hoots Barry.

Coach frowns. I'm not sure he agrees with me on that, but there's no time to change it.

"You can do this!" I shake my fists triumphantly. "Onward soldiers!" I cry.

"Onward soldiers!" Hattie shouts, joined by Cathy and Hugh, Lizzie and Diego, until they're all cheering the battle cry.

Coach's bottom lip peels down, and he pats me on the back. "Good try lad. Let's see if it makes a difference."

The team jogs out to their positions. I run after Hattie and say "score some goals!" I give her a friendly squeeze on the shoulder, but it's an order rather than a suggestion. "This is the day for your hat trick."

As the team spreads out, I notice that Fergus is still sitting on the ground, his head between his knees. I dart back to the goalmouth.

"Fergus, did you hear what I was saying? We're going on the attack."

He puffs, pushing himself off the ground.

I stand in front of him. "You do realise that if it wasn't for your super saves in the first half, we wouldn't have a chance in the second." I pick his gloves off the ground and slap them into his hands. "You are my first-half hero, because you have given us an opportunity."

He pulls his goalie gloves back on, looking at me steadily. "You mean that?"

I stare straight into his grass-green eyes. "Yes! We can win this, Fergus."

"OK." Fergus thumps a fist into a gloved hand and stamps his boots into the ground. "You don't have to worry about me, Barney. No more balls are getting past."

41: BELIEF

Within minutes of the kick off, Hattie collects the ball. She flicks it on for Hugh, who makes a storming run down the left. He lays it off to Hattie, now speeding down the centre. She slips the ball back to Hugh, who quickly chips it over the defender into the box. The keeper comes off his line towards the ball but Hattie sprints faster and nutmegs the goalie.

"Goal! Goal!" Our supporters go wild. Across the pitch, I can see Dad hugging Mum, trying to lift her off the ground. How embarrassing.

"Great start!" I yell.

Wasting no time, the guys race back to their starting positions. Ten minutes later, Lizzie boots a long ball over Vijay's head towards the attackers. Rocket power fires Cathy's little legs into action. She motors up the pitch, faster than a Jack Russell, knocking defenders from her path. She takes a shot! The goalie jumps high and manages to get a finger to it.

"Ooooh!" gasps the crowd as the ball hits the crossbar and bounces back, over the defenders, towards the edge of the box. Hattie, tracking the deflection, strikes an amazing volley back at the goal. The goalkeeper can't react quickly enough.

"Goal! Goal! Goal!" Al, Barry and I jump around like crazy.

We've drawn level, two all.

"Onward Soldiers!" cries Grandpa, hopping from one foot to the other. He nearly bursts my eardrums.

Coach bounces up and down the line. "I can't believe it!" he says as he springs past. "Come on! We can win this!"

Al nudges me. "Blimey, you've even made him positive."

The clock ticks on and it's time for a change. Our strategy has become too predictable. There are now defenders glued to both Cathy and Hugh. We can no longer reach them. Vijay was thriving on mentoring Angus, but with the ball hanging around in midfield he's beginning to panic.

"Vijay's losing the plot," I say loudly when Coach stands in front of me. "He's missing so many tackles."

"Yeah, you're right," Al agrees.

Coach turns to the bench. "Al, start warming up!" he orders.

Barry and I jog up and down with Al and stop to do a few stretches down near our goal. Lunging right, then left, Al winces.

"How's your ankle?" I ask.

"Sore." He rotates his foot.

Time is running out for either side to score a winner but we are in the danger zone. An attack is imminent.

"Wake up Eddie!" I holler. Amazingly, Eddie sprints out, making a crucial tackle. The ball flies off the back line for a corner.

"Ref! Ref! Substitution!" shouts Coach. He waves at us to return. "Vijay, you're off." Scowling, Vijay drags his feet off the pitch. "Well played, lad. Now Al, go get us that winner."

Corner kick. All the opposing players are in the box except the goalkeeper. Even Hugh and Cathy are running back to defend.

"Pick a player!" I yell. I can't help myself.

I look for Hattie but can't spot her amongst all the bodies piled into the box. I hope she keeps watching for spaces. The ball curls up to the top of the box, where their striker appears unmarked! Eddie, where *are* you!

The striker takes a tap and shoots high. Fergus, our goalie, leaps into the air and punches the ball out left.

"Fantastic Fergus!"

Al scoops the ball up and nudges it wide to Olive, who boots it far up field into open space.

The opposition battle to get back but already sprinting at warp speed up field is Hattie Frank! The Harlimac Harrier controls the ball with her right foot, dribbling fast towards the goal. On the other side of the pitch, Dad is running down the sideline, punching the air.

"Go, Hattie! Go!" Grandpa is yelling.

"Hat trick!" Barry bellows.

Three of the opposition race after her, closing her down. Driving into the box, it's the Harlimac Harrier versus the goalkeeper. The goalie's coming off his line.

"Chip it! Shoot!" Screams fly from the crowd as we can see the opposition on her heels catching her up.

Planting her left foot on the ground, Hattie draws back her right to strike. Simultaneously, two feet slide in behind her, the studs digging up grass and smashing into the Harlimac Harrier's ankle.

"Aargh!"

A piercing screech of the referee's whistle and Hattie's cry of pain silences the crowd.

"Noooo!" Dad wails, clutching his head. "Penalty Ref!"

Coach runs on with water bottles and a first aid kit.

My sister slumps on the grass just inside the box, a casualty of the opposing centre back - a nippy little character with a vicious glare and knobbly knees.

"No way was he ever going for the ball," complains Barry.

A red card is drawn swiftly from the referee's pocket. The centre back is off. Another screech from the ref's whistle, and he points to the penalty spot. Hattie's still down. Dad is jogging along the back of the pitch over to our side with Mum in hot pursuit, doing a very fast walk.

"Hattie's not up," Grandpa looks on, rubbing his chin.

My sister lies on the ground whilst Coach surveys the damage.

"Last kick of the game and we've got a penalty!" Dad arrives, rubbing his hands together.

"Oh no, my baby's hurt," Mum gasps, slapping Dad on the arm.

"Stop fussing!" grumbles Dad.

"She normally just jumps up and races on," says Mum, watching Coach carefully as he helps Hattie stand on one leg. Mum presses her clasped fingers to her lips. Grandpa puts a comforting arm across her shoulders.

"Come on, Hattie, be brave!" Dad shouts through cupped hands. "Let's get this penalty."

Pointing to the spot, Coach looks at Hattie, but the Harlimac Harrier shakes her head. He issues instructions that we can't hear.

Cathy hands Al the ball. As Coach helps Hattie hobble off the pitch, Al shifts the ball from hand to hand, but he's looking towards us, his face all screwed up. He bends down and rubs his ankle.

"Barry, quick, take your tracksuit off, look ready to go on as Hattie's replacement," I tell him.

"Me? What about you?" He unzips his jacket.

"You're a great shot when the ball is still," I say.

"I've never played for the first team." He stamps down his tracksuit bottoms onto the grass.

"Now's your chance."

Coach arrives supporting Hattie. Mum suffocates her in a hug.

"Give her your jacket," Mum orders Dad. "We've got to keep her warm."

"Barry's ready to take her place, sir." I push him forward.

"You?" Coach pauses. "Go on then, take a position at the back, there's less than a minute left." He waves Barry on, then turns to the injured Hattie.

Bent down, rubbing his own ankle, Al sets the ball on the grass.

"What's wrong with Al?" Grandpa asks me.

"I think his ankle's still weak. Al!" I call. He looks up. "Barry's on!" I point in Barry's direction as he strides across the turf.

"Barry!" Al beckons him over, picks up the ball and hands it to our big friend.

Barry's beaming. He waddles like a penguin to place the ball on the penalty spot.

"What's going on?" Coach stands up just as Barry is preparing to shoot. "Why isn't Al taking the penalty?"

151

Knees bent, arms wide, the goalkeeper settles into a squat and signals with one hand to the ref that he's ready.

"Sore ankle," Grandpa informs Coach. "But this boy's solid. I've heard it on good authority."

Coach slaps his cheeks and bares his teeth. It's too late to make a change.

Barry takes four mighty steps back from the ball and nods to the ref.

The whistle blows.

His bulky body sucks in a deep breath.

Legs the size of tree trunks plod on the spot. He winds his forearms around in tiny circles, building momentum. "Flying footballs!" he yells, and fires into action.

Barry's big boot strikes. The goalkeeper sinks to the floor as the ball is blasted over his shoulder into the back of the net.

"Goal!"

Barry's arms fly out like the wings of a plane. He scoops Al into the air. A final whistle peeps across the pitch. The team is jumping and screaming.

"We won!"

"Yes! Yes!" Dad invades the pitch, carrying Hattie in his arms.

"Oh yeah! Oh yeah! We're the winners!" Vijay and I dance on the bench.

Dad's parading around the ground with Hattie on his shoulders. Mum is crying. Grandpa offers her his handkerchief. I stand up to join them.

"We are the champions!" I sing. Grandpa pulls me close. He wipes a tear from his baggy eyes. "Are you crying, Grandpa?"

"No, it's the cold," he claims. Holding me tight in one arm, he looks down at me and says. "Well done, Barney."

I won't ever forget this day.

42: I CAN'T DO ANYTHING RIGHT

"I want the gold boots," moans Hattie, stomping into the kitchen. She crashes down onto the chair, laying her head on the table and covering it with her arms.

"They didn't fit." Dad's unsympathetic. Two hours trawling through every sports shop in town trying on football boots has taken its toll.

"Oh dear." Mum fills the kettle.

Dad chucks his keys and wallet onto the side. He stands at the window rubbing his eyes and yawning. I think he needs more than a mug of tea. "The black and white pair in the first shop were the best fit," he states.

"I don't want black and white boots. I want gold boots so that I stand out on the pitch!"

"To stand out on the pitch?" repeats Mum.

"Yeah, apparently it's all about the colour and nothing to do with your level of skill," I explain. I'm being sarcastic.

"Shut up, Barney!" snaps Hattie, flinging back her head. "Just coz you didn't get to play." She stands up and limps out of the kitchen.

"That's not very nice," I complain as I hear Hattie hobbling up the stairs.

"Neither was your remark," says Mum firmly.

"Aren't you going to tell her off?" I ask Dad.

"Just leave it will you, Barney," he snaps.

I feel my insides boiling like the kettle. Mum pours the hot water into the teapot. I can't hold my feelings in any more. I overflow.

"It's not fair!" I erupt. "She gets away with everything because you think she's the best! She's spoilt!"

"That's enough, Barney. I said leave it!" Dad raises his voice and thumps his fist on the table.

"I'm out of here!" I storm off to my room.

Lying on my bed I can hear Hattie weeping next door. I tiptoe outside her room and peek through the gap. She's laying out all her sports kit and training shoes on the floor. Her favourite boots that she wore for the final are shiny and clean. Why does she need new boots anyway? I'm right, she *is* just spoilt.

She sits down on the carpet, resting her head against the bed, and picks up one of the clean boots. She slips her hand inside the shoe and pokes her finger through a hole in the bottom. Her finger wriggles like a worm poking out of the ground. Now I *really* feel guilty. I retreat to my room.

Am I jealous of my sister?

***

Five times I got Grandpa to check his emails this afternoon but we still haven't heard anything from the TV show. Worse than that, we don't have any ideas for the training machine either. Help!

Nobody talks during supper. The clink of cutlery against the plates seems to echo around the room.

Dad is first to break the silence. "Put your wings in, Barney!" He pushes down my bent elbows. I rest them on the table. "Don't put your elbows on the table!"

I can't do anything right.

Wisely, Grandpa chose to eat supper in his annex. I think I might visit him when I've finished. I might feel more welcome there.

"I've been thinking, Hattie, about the new boots." Dad scratches his nose. My sister slices into her meat. "Football's finished now, so how about we wait until the new season starts." Dad rests his elbow on the table and waves his fork in the air. Can you believe it? It's all right for him to do that but I'm not allowed. "Your feet will probably grow over the summer and there'll be lots of new styles to choose from." Dad eats his last mouthful and places his cutlery together on his empty plate. His arm pushes on the table, balancing his chair back on two legs – another thing I'm not supposed to do. He waits for Hattie to answer.

"I guess it's a good idea to wait if my feet are still growing, and my ankle's still a bit swollen," she says, hoping for the sympathy vote.

"Think yourself lucky. I'm not being offered new things." I swallow quickly to get my point in. Sticking my chin out, I try to look hurt.

"Mum bought you new clothes the other day because you've grown out of your others," Hattie reminds me. Mum looks up, narrowing her eyes and smiling at me. Hattie complained at the time, but obviously Mum couldn't tell her the real reason why we went shopping.

Anyhow, that's different because I didn't actually ask for those.

***

When I walk into Grandpa's annex, he's driving the Flying Scotsman into the station, where a collection of characters is waiting.

"Glad you're here, Barney, we need to bounce a few ideas about for this training machine," he says.

"Do you *have* any ideas?" I ask.

He doesn't reply immediately. I listen to the trains whirring along the track. You have to be patient while Grandpa's thinking. Sometimes I imagine all the wheels and cogs turning inside his brain. He's like a valuable antique, a precious collectable that churns through information in minute detail. Today's processing is particularly slow, and I watch the Flying Scotsman complete ten laps of the circuit before he answers.

"No, not a single one," he finally admits.

I plop myself down onto a stool, accidentally nudging his hand on the control dial. One train speeds around the bend and de-rails.

"Ooh, sorry about that." I stand back to avoid knocking anything else. I seem to be getting clumsier by the day.

Grandpa rolls his eyes. "Relax, Barney," he replies. "It doesn't matter. Now, this machine, we need to think in 3D," he suggests. "Or 4D even."

"4D?"

"Sounds and feelings," said Grandpa, "the crowd cheering. It could be raining, windy, who knows."

"Perhaps we need wind machines and shower sprays," I suggest. "Or do you think that's going to be too expensive?"

Grandpa thinks for a moment. Tapping his pencil on the table, he says, "Yes. On second thoughts, perhaps we should just concentrate on the basic principle of the feet reaction times."

I blow up my cheeks and let the air hiss out slowly. This is such a difficult task. *Can I really do this?*

43: BIG ANNOUNCEMENT

The next afternoon, Grandpa is walking down the garden path as I get home from school. He looks twitchy. "You're home." Now he's stating the obvious.

"Yes we are." I step out to hug him but he goes to open the car boot instead.

"Hurry up and come on in then. I'll help with the school bags and the shopping."

"Thanks," says Mum, as she wanders down the side of the car.

Loaded with bags and coats, Grandpa is already trotting back up the path. "Good day?" he calls without waiting for a response.

Mum stops and stares after Grandpa, watching him disappear into the house.

"Is he acting a bit odd?" I ask Mum.

She turns back to the boot and hands me a large pack of loo roll. "Put these in the cupboard under the stairs please, Barney."

I'm just stuffing the pack between the ironing board and the hoover when I hear, "Pssst!"

I pop my head back around the door.

"Barney, this way." I can hear Grandpa but I can't see him. I follow the sound of his voice into the kitchen. "Hurry up." I catch a glimpse of his feet disappearing up the annex staircase. I race after him.

"I've been waiting for you all day," he says as I walk into his annex.

He sits down at his desk, beckoning me over to the computer screen.

"Are you all right, Grandpa? You seem a bit...odd."

I wander over. I look at his weathered face and all the tiny folds and bristles. He takes a quick glance back in the direction of the stairs, checking that no one has followed us.

"We've had another email," he blurts. Waves of goose bumps are popping up along my arms as I read from the screen.

Speechless, we collapse onto his small sofa.

Moments later, Mum appears wielding a feather duster. "You two have gone very pale," she remarks, polishing the desk. Simultaneously we point to the computer. Mum nudges the mouse, and the email flashes back onto the screen. She reads it out loud.

"Your training machine designs must be submitted by 5pm Friday. The Premiership's Football Manager Show will be aired Saturday at 7pm. At the end of the show you will find out whether or not you are through to the live finals."

Mum spins to face us, her mouth open so wide you could fit an apple in whole. "Wow! How exciting!" She skips over and pokes me with the feather duster. "What's the matter then?"

Silently Grandpa nods. "The day of reckoning," he says. He holds his chin in one hand, pushing his fingers into his jaw and making his cheeks look chubby. "Knowing whether you're in or out."

"So the design of our training machine is crucial."

A beeper sounds from Mum's apron.

"Oh, that'll be my cake baked." She delves into the front pocket, stopping the alarm. "Honestly, what a pair!" she laughs. "I'll leave you TV stars to muse over your fate." Dancing away, Mum stops by the door and looks back. "I think it's about time we told your father."

I've been dreading this moment.

***

"My boy on TV?"

A steaming chicken curry sits on the plate in front of Dad, but his knife and fork remain glued to the table.

"Did you really meet Reggie Hunter?" Hattie is showing me the entire contents of her mouth.

"My boy a football manager?" Dad's voice vibrates.

"Did you actually shake his hand?"

"Hattie, manners," Mum scolds. "Close your mouth whilst you're eating! How many times do I have to tell you?"

"The Football Manager Show on TV?" Dad is gawping at Grandpa and me on the opposite side of the table.

My face muscles ache as I try not to giggle. I stuff a forkful of rice into my mouth to mask my smile.

"I want to come to the next filming," squawks Hattie, slamming her cutlery into the table.

"Sorry, Hattie, it's just Barney and me for now I'm afraid," says Grandpa.

"That's not fair!" She plunges her fork into a stalk of broccoli and ferociously bites the end off.

Dad's plateful is still untouched. His face is frozen.

"Your food's going cold, love." Mum gently pats his arm.

His bottom lip begins to quiver and his droopy eyes are welling up. "Our son is going to be on TV," he croaks. He pushes back his chair and walks around the table, smothering me with his long arms.

"I'm so proud," he sobs on my shoulder. "I'm so very, very proud."

I want to laugh and cry at the same time.

44: HELP

I wasn't planning on telling anyone else about my TV debut, but by the end of registration everyone at school seems to know.

"Hattie reckons you're going to be on the Premiership's Football Manager Show." Al races to catch up with me as I walk down the corridor. Other kids move out of my way. Small groups mutter to each other behind their hands as I pass. "How did you get tickets to go and watch?"

"Barney, I heard you're gonna be on the TV. Is it true?" Vijay walks out of his class to ask me, followed by Lizzie and Olive.

"Did you really meet Reggie Hunter?"

I'm trying to answer but everyone is asking questions all at once. Most of the team is now circling me.

"You never!"

"Why are you on TV?"

"Coz he got tickets to go and watch! Why do you think?"

We're creating a traffic jam, and the call for the first lesson will be any minute.

"Stop!" I hold my hand up in the air. "Team meeting in the goalmouth at first break. Be there if you want to know more."

The bell rings above our heads, and chattering kids flood out of their classrooms.

***

A fine drizzle means we are the only ones daft enough to be sitting out on the field, perfect for my announcement.

"Yes, I am going to be on the Premiership's Football Manager Show."

"I knew it," says Al to Diego, sat beside him. "I told you he got tickets."

"I'm not watching the show, I'm..."

"What?" Erica squeals so high it hurts my ears. "Do they coach you to play footie then?"

Lizzie bends forward and touches my hand.

"What are you doing?" I pull my hand away.

"I'm touching the hand that shook the hand of Reggie Hunter," Lizzie says.

Erica pounces at me. I sidestep and hide behind Al, dodging out of her reach. She leans over and starts sniffing me. "Have you washed since? Coz if I'd shaken Reggie's hand I'd never wash ever again."

Hattie is in hysterics.

"Of course he's washed," Al says. "Girls, get a grip, control yourselves and sit down. Let's listen to what they taught him."

The team take their places around the goalmouth. Finally I can sit down without being poked.

"No one teaches me anything on the show."

They all stare at me, faces drooping, disappointed.

"I am a contestant. I am the manager, or I might be anyway."

"Flying footballs," whistles Eddie, blowing a bogie off the top of his finger.

"How come they let you on the show?" sneers Vijay. He still hasn't forgiven me for his substitution in the final.

"Because he's the best." Barry stands up next to me. He's grown so tall this year that the top of my head barely reaches his armpit.

"Did you win?" asks Diego.

"It's only the first round!" Hattie bursts out. I can't believe she lasted this long before spilling more details.

"More importantly, I need your help. I have to design a training machine to perfect a skill and I want your ideas."

Silence. Oh dear.

"Have a think and write anything good down and put it in my locker by the end of today. Think about skills you use in other sports too."

The bell goes for the end of break. The guys start getting up.

Erica breathes down my neck like a sniffer dog. "Can I meet Reggie Hunter if I help you?" she growls.

"Possibly." I step away.

"See ya later Barney." She waves her fingers at me, then runs off giggling with the other girls.

"Have you met Agrovio?" asks Hogger Hugh.

"No, I haven't..."

"He's brilliant," Al butts in.

"He's my favourite player," says Diego. "Got a poster of him on my wall."

"Yeah, me too," Angus joins in.

The four boys head off towards school, discussing the best goals they've seen Agrovio score. Shame he hasn't scored any this season!

"I'm sure I'll have some good ideas later," Vijay assures me before he leaves.

Eddie wants to shake my hand but I know where those fingers have been most of the morning so I make it quick. Happy Barry is the only one left, sitting on the field staring into space.

"Darts!" he booms. "Aim and fire!" he says very seriously. "I liked your hula-hoop target practice too."

"Thanks for that, Barry, I can write that down."

"No problem Barney...the manager." He gets up and slaps me on the back. I know he's being playful but he's so heavy handed, I'm winded. "Heh, what were the lunches like? Bet you got loads of great stuff."

Of all the things he could ask me, he's just interested in the grub.

***

Hattie and I kneel on the rug in Grandpa's annex. She empties the contents of the bag in a pile at Grandpa's feet.

He's sitting in his armchair, holding a mug of hot chocolate. "Read them out then, Barney," he instructs, "so we can divide them into good and not so good ideas."

One by one, I pick out the folded pieces of paper and read the suggestions made by the team.

"A diving machine – Fergus."

"It'd help the goalkeeper but not the rest of us," Hattie complains, putting it straight onto the 'not so good' pile.

"Worth considering though. Goalkeepers are important in any team."

Hattie reads the next idea. "Diego thinks it could be like ten pin bowling for football."

"That's quite good." I point to the good pile.

Hattie picks up another slip of paper. "A football-striking machine to make your kicking and passing stronger – Al, Angus and Hugh."

"That's all right," says Grandpa, shuffling forward in his seat to look over her shoulder. "Good pile, don't you think?"

"Yeah I like that one," I agree.

"Eddie – tackle bag," Hattie reads.

"Tackle bag – what does that even mean? I thought you used a tackle bag in rugby."

"He probably got confused as usual. Shall I screw it up?" asks Hattie, curling the paper in her hands.

"No, put it on the 'not sure' pile."

I unfold another idea. "Dance machine – Hattie." I look at her. She grins, patting the 'good' pile beside her.

I'm still holding her note when she begins reading out Erica's suggestion. "Dance is a great way to get fit and learn fancy footwork," she says. She passes the note to Grandpa. "Isn't that funny, Erica had the same idea as me." As if the two of them have never discussed it.

"Lizzie – a dance machine to get people moving." I pretend to be surprised.

"It must be a good idea if three of us think so," says Hattie. She plucks the note from my hand and reads it again like she didn't know what it was going to say.

"Amazing that Lizzie thought of a machine about moving. Maybe she's realising her weaknesses," I say.

Hattie unwraps another note. "Cathy – a fast-moving dance machine."

"To get those little legs motoring." I giggle.

"Shall I put all four of them on the good pile?" Hattie's hand hovers.

"Go on then."

Two folded notes are left. I pick the largest one. "Vijay – crikey, he's written an essay."

"He's so clever, Vijay; everything he does is planned out," drones Hattie. "He's going to be a dentist."

I hand it over to Grandpa. He reads faster than I do. "A balancing machine. Put one big peg in the ground with a hole in it like a needle. Thread a very long piece of elastic through it. Tie the two ends of elastic to two separate players. Throw balls for the players to kick. Only one player can kick the ball at a time, so if one goes forward, the other goes back."

"The balancing act! He remembers what I asked to him to do at the final." And I thought he didn't like me.

"Your coaching skills are working." Grandpa ruffles his hand in my hair. "Let's see who's left." He bends to collect up the last note. "Olive," he reads, smiling.

"Let me guess. What might Hattie's new friend write?" I glare at my sister.

"A little bit difficult to read, more of a picture." Grandpa's eyebrows wiggle about his forehead. "You might want to look at this yourself." He pushes the note into my hand.

"It'll be dance won't it, Hattie?"

"OK, I admit it." Hattie holds up her hands. "We all agreed a dance machine would be perfect." Hattie shuffles the 'good' pile. I quickly stuff Olive's note into my pocket, having glanced at it. "Basically, you need to design a machine like a dance mat, or bowling alley, that gets you moving around and striking the ball really hard." I hang my head down and pretend to be studying the notes until my cheeks stop burning. "Or you've got Vijay's idea," Hattie continues. "But you need two players for that."

"Yeah, might be too complicated," I croak. I cough, my voice sounds funny. "I think it's supposed to be for individual players. What do you think, Grandpa?" I ask, still keeping my head down.

"I think we should go with the majority, mixing the four boys' idea of the striking machine with the girls' dance mat."

"Right." I start gathering up all the notes. "I'll take these to my room and get designing. Thanks for your help Hattie." I exit swiftly.

***

The training machine is taking shape but it's not amazing yet. It's late. I need to sleep and rest my brain. Maybe I'll be inspired by a dream.

I flatten out the screwed up note on my desk and read it again.

Idea - A dance game to help footwork skills. Olive xxx
PS Thanks for giving us the best team talk ever.

She's drawn a little love heart too. I feel a bit wobbly. I fold the note up neatly and hide it in my secret box before jumping into bed.

45: INSPIRATION

We have to deliver our design for the training machine to Broadcasting Base today. It's make or break.

"Shall I click send?" asks Grandpa, peering at me over the top of his spectacles. One press of a button and my whole life could change. If I win, I'll be mingling with millionaire footballers, invited to spend the weekends on their yachts and eat as many ice creams as I want. But it's a big 'if', and one that'll involve dealing with some big egos and demanding fans.

"Let's just go over it one more time." Something's niggling me about our entry. The team's ideas were really useful, and Hattie's helped a lot, especially in explaining how a dance mat works. But is it good enough? Are we really up to the test?

"Shall I read out our worksheet once again?" Grandpa offers as I sit blowing the corner of the worksheet until it slides off the desk.

Grandpa leans down to retrieve it. "Might help to put your mind at rest. You just sit and listen," he suggests.

"OK, thanks."

"Our training machine is designed to improve the speed and accuracy of a player's reaction on the ball." He pauses, pushes his glasses up his nose and continues. "The basic idea consists of a flat mat with eight coloured footballs spaced around the edge of a large circle. In the centre of the mat is a black square, where the player stands. Each football has a small, coloured fibre-optic light embedded within it that will go on and off at random."

Grandpa clears his throat. "The player must kick each football as it lights up, returning to the centre square after each kick. The speed of the lights changing can be increased as the player improves."

"Stop!" I snap, jumping up from my chair and pacing the room. The cuff of my sweatshirt is soggy with spit where I've been chewing it. "It's not right; it's faulty. What if he kicks the ball and breaks the light? And it doesn't use the bowling alley idea really."

"Barney, it's a prototype. There'll be time to adjust it once they decide to make it," says Grandpa.

"I don't think they'll want to make it," I sigh. "It's not dynamic enough."

"Simple can be good sometimes, Barney. Don't over-complicate things." Grandpa's knobbly fingers hover over the keyboard.

I reach out and move his hand away from the 'send' button.

"I know but it's just a dance mat with footballs on, not a football-training mat. It doesn't make your kicking any harder, like the boys suggested."

I pick the printed sample from his hand. Scratching my head, I can't even focus on the writing. We're running out of time.

"Barney!" Hattie yells from downstairs, making Grandpa wince. "Barney!"

"What?" I bark, walking to the annex entrance. "Don't press 'send' just yet, Grandpa," I plead, before jogging down the steps.

"Do you want this? I'm having a clear out and I found it in my room." Hattie stands at the bottom of the stairs holding a small orange box. "Mum says it was a present to you on your first birthday." A statement that means *you should cherish this until you are 99 and then give it to your grandchildren as an antique.*

I pluck it from her outstretched hand. "Thanks." I begin to climb back upstairs. "What is it?" I turn around but she's already gone.

Grandpa waits patiently, sipping his tea. "What have you got there, Barney?"

I flip the small golden hook that holds down the lid.

Pop! The box jumps, I jump and Grandpa jumps. A clown with a big red nose wearing an old Harlimac football strip bursts out.

"Damn jack-in-a-box," Grandpa groans. "I've spilt my tea." He starts dabbing at the mess with a tissue.

"Oh, now I remember, it was my first present from Dad." I snap the lid shut and let it pop up again. I keep repeating it; even though I know the jack is going to spring out, I can't predict exactly when, so I jump every time.

"That's it!" I cry. "Jack-in-a-box, Grandpa!" I squeal. I slap the jack down and release him again.

"Yes Barney, I know what it is," he replies, still mopping up his tea.

"We need to make the mat like a 3D jack-in-a-box."

Grandpa stares back. "You've lost me."

I rub my forehead. "The balls need to pop up. A player has to dance around to actually kick the balls."

"I hope we don't get sued for damages when Maxime Buti twists his ankle dancing on our machine!" Grandpa drops his pencil onto the pad.

Elbows on the table, I rest my chin in my hands. I'm concentrating.

"I think it's got potential," I say after a long pause. I hop up and start pacing the room again. "We need to make it dynamic."

Grandpa picks up his pencil and doodles a simple picture of a circle with a series of dots around the circumference. He adds arrows pointing out from each dot. It reminds me of Barry's idea of firing darts.

"What if we reverse the arrows?" I point to his drawing. Crouching beside him I explain. "What if the balls are held around the edge of a circle and anyone of them could fire into play inside the circle at anytime?"

"I think we've sown a seed, Barney." He reverses the arrows pointing them back into the circle, sits back and admires his drawing.

"We'll make sure it's practical," I assure him. "What if it measures how hard the player kicks the ball?"

"You could use a Newton meter to gauge force." Grandpa is so clever.

I stand in front of his train track, admiring the scenery - the small details of his work, like the picket fence on a garden, the trucks full of bundles of twigs acting as tree trunks, waiting to be transported by the 'shunter'.

"Grandpa, I've got it!" I pick up the 'shunter' from the track and spin around to face him firing up the lights and the sound of a roaring crowd. "How about a virtual screen as the target. We could have flying dart boards to fire at, with top marks for a bull's-eye." I walk across the room firing an imaginary dart. "Players would have to use their peripheral vision to look out for balls entering the circle or...or..." I suddenly find myself trotting on the spot and clapping excitedly. I think it's a girl thing I've picked up off Hattie.

"It's all coming together," cheers Grandpa as he busily scribbles down notes.

"Or the ball could call out their name."

Grandpa's hand hesitates on the page. "We can work on that one."

***

Throughout the afternoon, Grandpa feeds us with chocolate biscuits and waters us with juice. Gradually our concept grows. We try out a variety of styles, using screwed up paper balls to test out our ideas, booting paper all over the annex until it looks like there's been a giant hailstorm. Finally, it's time to blossom.

"Barney Frank's Training Tool – The Shunter." My heart is beating fast. Just checking the document gives me goosebumps. It reads:

'A large platform houses footballs around its edge. In the centre of the platform is a picture of a 'shunter' train, where the player stands. The player must respond to any football shunted into play from the edge of the platform, by retrieving the ball and kicking it towards a target projected on a virtual screen. They must return to stand on the centre shunter after each shot. A Newton meter hidden in the mesh backstop behind the virtual screen will measure the force of each kick.

The balls may roll, bounce or be passed at speed into play. Players may have to shoot or chip to hit the target.

The ball may roll in silently, or a whistle from the shunted ball may alert the player. This means that the player can be alerted by both sight and sound. The platform size can be adjusted to change the distance the player has to lunge or run to kick the ball. The speed of the test can also be altered.

The virtual screen can show either bull's-eye targets, moving players or a goal and goalkeeper at which to shoot. Once the balls pass through the virtual screen they are collected by the mesh backstop.

The key to this machine is to use peripheral vision; to be aware of what is going on around you and react quickly once movement is detected.'

To add to the description, I scan in a few of our sketches. I've even designed a 'shunter' logo.

"A fantastic machine!" Grandpa declares, holding up his hand for a high five. "We're on to a winner."

"It's not fantastic, it's 'Franktastic'!" We laugh. "Press 'send'."

In an instant all our work flies into cyberspace with a swoosh.

46: WHERE'S MY SUPPORT?

Mum sits with a box of tissues on her lap. On the floor I'm struggling to stay still. A hundred worms are wriggling in my tummy.

"I can't believe you didn't tell me you were meeting Reggie Hunter. You could've taken my football for him to sign." Hattie's head dangles upside down in front of me. "Whilst we're talking about autographs," she continues, "Lizzie wants her school shirt signed and so does Olive."

"Give him a chance," says Dad, easing himself into the armchair. "He's not even through yet."

I know Dad's right but does he have to be so blunt? He could've said '*when* he gets through…'

"The Premiership's Football Manager Show!" The theme tune blasts out of the television. My thumbs are twiddling uncontrollably as I watch the clips of Harlimac FC scoring goals. They must've gone back years to find these.

"Sit over here, Barney." Dad pats the arm of his chair. "Come on, son."

He never asks me normally. I shuffle over, and he pulls a cushion out from beneath him for me to lean against.

"You're going to be on TV, son." He messes my hair. "You're gonna be on TV!"

"There!" Hattie points at the TV. "I spy you." The images are flashing up so quick I can't even spot myself. "Were you wearing pink?"

"No!"

"I knew I should've worn my gold suit." Combing his silver hair with his fingers, Grandpa perches on the edge of his seat, awaiting his TV debut.

"You'd definitely be easy to see then," says Mum, grinning at me.

I shake my head and give her a cross-eyed stare. Don't encourage him, just in case we *do* get through.

"It's Reggie Hunter!" Hattie jumps up, waving her Harlimac shirt at the television.

He introduces Rachel Wise and Lord Loadsa.

"Was she there at your filming?" asks Dad, his bristly face close to mine.

"Yes, they were all there."

"Was she dressed like that?" Tonight she is squeezed into a long red dress, so tight I'm surprised she can breathe. Dad's dribbling. Ugh!

"No, she had a navy suit on. She looked much smarter, didn't she, Grandpa?" I turn towards him, away from drooling Dad.

"Yes, very professional. Not a party dress like that."

Reggie explains that the clips will be shown in order of the heats.

"Which were you?" asks Dad.

"Heat two."

Heat one fails miserably. One man is sacked and sent off stage for swearing at Reggie. They bleep it out. Another guy sits dead still whenever the panel ask a question. The camera keeps flicking back to him not moving.

"Stage fright, poor fella," Mum says. So far no need for tissues.

"If they're all like that, surely you must be in with a chance," laughs Dad. Makes me feel more confidence as I watch. Shame Dad didn't say, 'you're great compared to these guys'.

Suddenly Hattie screams. "It's you!"

Seeing Grandpa and me sitting at our desk sends my stomach into somersaults. I look pale on the screen, like I've seen a ghost.

"You look so smart," wails Mum. She's off, tissues at the ready.

The camera scrolls along the other contestants, past Bill Costly and the ref lady, all the way down to José.

"Wow! Someone wants to be noticed," comments Hattie when José's silver suit shines into view.

The shot rolls forward to José arguing with Reggie about the length of time given to the ref lady. They even show him using his mobile.

"They can't pick him, he's a cheat," says Hattie.

A funny sequence cuts back and forwards between the ref lady and Reggie as they try to understand her complicated game. It's cut from Reggie scratching his head to Rachel mouthing 'what?' and Lord Loadsa nodding off.

"That didn't happen!" I giggle. "I didn't see him fall asleep, did you, Grandpa?" When I glance over the coffee table, Grandpa pretends to be snoozing too.

"It's what older gentlemen do," Hattie says.

Bill Costly is explaining his football tennis.

"I think they'll choose him, they liked that idea."

But where are we?

My chin drops onto my knees. Have we been cut?

Now the screen is filled with papers flying across the floor in slow motion, sad music playing in the background and poor Fred Hooper crying, "It's all been a big mistake!"

"I feel sorry for Fred." But really it's myself I feel sorry for - we've barely been mentioned. I bet they put Bill Costly through instead of us.

"Poor chap couldn't handle the pressure," pipes Grandpa, "got himself in a right state." He takes a sip of his coffee and almost spits it straight out as the camera zooms in on me.

I sit bolt upright.

"Young Barnaby," Rachel Wise says, "not only came second in his fantasy league, he ranks in the top fifty nationally."

The camera is still on my face. I can barely watch. I spread my fingers out across my eyes and peep through the slits. They've edited out the full view of my braces – phew!

"What a shame you sold Vanson before the last game," Ms Wise purrs.

And that's it. It cuts back to Bill in dispute with Buti.

"Maxime Buti!" hollers Hattie. She thumps me on the arm. "You never told me you'd met him!" I flinch from the punch and suddenly see myself instructing Maxime in French.

Dad turns up the volume.

"Le feu…" I'm rubbing my belly. "La jambe…" I'm lifting my leg. "Le pied…" I flex my foot.

Dad shuffles forward in his seat.

I repeat the lines under my breath. I am chanting, "World Cup, eight!" There's an echo on my voice so it booms out of the TV.

Buti blasts the ball into the top corner. Reggie, Rachel and Lord Loadsa rise up, clapping. Dad and Hattie leap into the air. I'm flooded with a warm feeling, as if the sun's just come out from behind the clouds. I might need one of Mum's tissues in a minute.

Hattie's chanting, "World cup! World cup!"

"My son taught Maxime Buti how to score." Dad picks me up, with great effort, and kisses me on both cheeks. "They've got to put you through," he says, his eyes glistening.

They cut to the next heat. I'm bouncing on my cushion now.

"Let's not get carried away," Grandpa warns. "We've got to see how this lot do."

We spend an agonising hour watching all the other heats. Group three and four aren't very good.

"I think you've got the winning ticket, Barney," Dad says after the clips. He snaps open a can of beer. "If that's all they've got to offer, my boy will win easily."

But that isn't all they have to offer. Heats five, six, seven and eight are packed full of impressive contestants. They're sharp, and their answers are detailed, drawing on notable coaching experiences. A few are managers of top non-league clubs, not professional, but nearly.

One lady, an army captain, gets Buti sweating on a demanding fitness drill. "That lady is really good, look at poor Maxime, he's exhausted," Mum says.

During the adverts Dad and Hattie create a list of favourites. But, where am I?

"Some of these guys are really impressive. This is going to be tough." Dad chews on his nails as contestants continue to impress. I shiver as the sun slips away again.

"We've seen hundreds of entries and we are ready to cut the list down to ten contestants for the live finals next week," Reggie declares. Low beating music builds in the background. "The judges' decision is final." The studio lights fix on Reggie and a golden envelope. The music hits a crescendo as he pulls out a list of names. "Our live finalists are… Howard Edmunds…"

"That's the non-league man you said you liked, Dad," cries Hattie.

"…George Wright." A picture of the contestant spins onto the screen.

"That's the man that trains the deaf team. I wanted him to go through," shouts Hattie. "He knows all these tricks to get people to signal to each other without shouting." She waves her hands at me. I've no idea what's she's trying to say. Why does no one seem to be championing Grandpa and me?

"…Jane Rose."

"The army lady! Yes!" Dad punches the air. "She deserves it, and Harlimac need to work on fitness and stamina, I've been saying that all season." *I've never heard him say that before.* "Good," he continues, slouching back in his chair. "They've picked the two I thought have the most potential."

What about me?

"And the man I chose too," pipes Hattie.

How can they all sit here choosing their favourites and not include me? I can't look at anyone. A cold fear creeps over my body, freezing my muscles. Announcing name after name, the sound of the TV becomes muffled as I curl into my cocoon. Just leave me here until the autumn, when this is all over.

"And finally ... from round two," my ears prick up, "Bill Costly..." I feel like I've been punched. "...you very nearly made it through but our judges have chosen Barnaby and Barney Frank."

Did I hear right?

"Yes! Yes! Yes!" Dad leapfrogs over me out of his seat.

"Barney!" Hattie belts about the room.

"Barney, my boy, you're in! You're in the live finals!" Dad lifts me off my feet and jigs me in the air like I'm a kid again.

Mum's in floods of tears, squeezing Grandpa.

Suddenly Dad drops me, opens the lounge window and bellows out to the street.

"My son Barney Frank is in the Premiership's Football Manager Show live finals!"

47: DAD'S ADVICE

Barnaby and Barney Frank - Your presence is required at Broadcasting Base for the Live Finals of The Premiership's Football Manager Show. Please find enclosed a map and timing details.

I read the letter more than twenty times a day. I pin it on the board by the fridge, where everyone can see it. One more sleep until it's all decided, one way or the other.

"You've gotta show them who's boss tomorrow, son." Every evening Dad's been offering me advice. "Don't let them intimidate you. They may be bigger than you but your ideas are good."

I wish he'd think of a more exciting word. What about amazing or fantastic? I guess he means that they're solid and will work. Or perhaps he doesn't think that they are as good as the other finalists' ideas. After all, he was championing the army lady and the non-league coach until I was picked.

"Don't stand for any arguing or messing about."

"I think I'll get an early night, just listen to some music in my room," I announce. I'm beginning to realise it was easier when no one else knew about my entry.

"Good tactics, son. Give that brain a rest," says Dad, pushing aside the football books he piled up on the table earlier. He moves to the sideboard and picks up a trophy from his collection. He huffs on the cup and polishes it with his sleeve.

"Good night, love." Mum kisses me on the forehead. "Sleep well."

"Think about how you're going to address the team..." Dad starts up again, following me across the kitchen, trophy in hand. "What are..."

Mum raises her arm like a barrier as I exit the kitchen, stopping Dad from leaving.

"Barney's going to bed now," she says softly.

***

It's my big day tomorrow. I'm hanging out my clothes for the show. I tuck the blade of Harlimac turf into my trouser pocket. Will I be able to control a team of men?

A quick knock on my bedroom door and in walks Hattie.

"I made you this." She hands me a braided bracelet with *Good luck* weaved in it. "That's a football." She points to a black and white dotted circle.

"Cool."

"You don't have to wear it on TV if you don't want. You could keep it in your pocket as a lucky charm." I slip it on as she studies me. "I think you've got a good chance of winning tomorrow," she says.

"Really?" I look up at her.

"Yeah, I do. You're different to the others."

I bite my lip.

185

She smiles. "That's a good thing Barney."

"Thanks."

"Goodnight. See you in the morning." She disappears, closing the door behind her.

"Night."

I hop into bed, still wearing the bracelet. I play the 'Stars Wars' theme tune because it takes me to a galaxy far, far away. That's what I need tonight.

48: THE SHUNTER

Backstage, Grandpa pulls off his scarf and unbuttons his smart jacket. He stands up and his jacket flaps open.

"What are you wearing?" I rub my eyes.

"I've customized a Harlimac football shirt. Do you like it?"

I'm not sure *like* is the right word…

A winged collar has been sewn around the neck, tied with a bright blue and red spotty bow tie, and a strip of silver buttons runs down the centre stripe.

"Just you wait till you see the sleeves." He chuckles.

"Barney and Barnaby Frank, you're up. Follow me." A man with headphones and a mouthpiece summons us into the studio just as the previous contestant is leaving. I swallow hard.

It's Hattie's favourite, the man who trains the deaf team. He holds a towel, patting his forehead. As we come level, I give him a thumbs up. In response, he draws a pointed finger sharply across his throat.

"Oh crikey!" says Grandpa, fiddling with his bow tie.

There is no place to hide now. The arena awaits.

***

"Maxime, this is an excellent demonstration." Grandpa thanks the player for trying out our training machine.

It feels like it's going well, so far...

I keep squinting at the audience, looking for Mum and Dad, but the lights are far too bright to see.

"Your reaction times to the ball improved by one second in the latter half of the practice, and your shots rose to ninety per cent accurate." I read the statistics from the machine, a proper working, automated, 'Shunter Machine'. It's weird to see it here, for real, in front of me.

Grandpa slips his hand in his jacket pocket, pulls out the 'shunter' that he brought along from his train set and places it next to the control box. Then he peels off his jacket and drapes it over his chair. In the studio lights the sleeves of his golden suit shimmer, cut from the original jacket and attached to the Harlimac shirt. Even the audience gasp. Oh dear.

"One, two," Grandpa calls, beating out each second with a clap. "It may not seem long, but it's all the time you need - to get to the ball first then to dribble away or offload."

"Time to aim and fire!" I repeat the words Barry used when he was talking about darts.

"Well done you guys." Reggie walks onto stage to cut us off. Perhaps Grandpa's jacket is too blinding on camera. I feel like my balloon's been popped. But then Reggie raises his clapping hands to the crowd. "Let's give it up for Barnaby and Barney!"

Sudden loud cheering amazes me. Even Buti joins in with the applause. I'm desperate to bow but not sure if that's the done thing.

Grandpa shakes the Frenchman's hand. Maxime then raises his palm for me to slap, live on air!

Maxime Buti walks off stage, and we're about to follow when Agrovio, Harlimac's centre forward, walks on. His head casts a shadow over me, blocking out the studio lights. The crowd goes wild. Agrovio's their hero. I don't understand why since he can't seem to score anymore.

"My turn," he says in a thick accent. He hunches over me, so close that it hurts my neck to look up at him.

I gulp. Reggie glances at the producer, who signals with his fingers.

"Go for it, Agrovio." Reggie backs away. He covers his microphone to tell me - "You've got two minutes."

"If you'd like to take your place on the 'Shunter', Mr Agrovio." I go to reset the machine.

"Don't look so worried, Mr Barney." I realise I'm not smiling anymore. "I think I will do well on your invention," Agrovio boasts as he strides over to the machine.

The platform creaks as Agrovio thumps his feet onto the 'Shunter Machine'. Beside me Grandpa checks the settings and confirms that we're ready to start.

The attacker rolls his head, cracks his knuckles and jogs on the spot. "Begin!" he orders.

Three short, sharp whistles signal the start of the practice, and the first ball pops up from the box. Agrovio lunges left to boot it. To begin with he strikes each ball at a good speed and hits the target ninety five per cent of the time. "I am doing Ok, huh?" he cackles. The crowd cheers. "This machine is too easy. Make it harder!"

Is he mocking my design?

I increase the speed by quite a bit. Immediately, Agrovio starts to falter, his swings getting wilder. He barely reaches a long ball out right. A whistle from his left should alert him to the next ball, but he's too slow, barely clipping it. His accuracy rate plummets.

An image of a player running across the pitch appears on the virtual screen. Agrovio doesn't notice. Snorting, he stamps his boot on the AstroTurf that covers the machine. Silently, a ball appears behind him, but he's no longer checking.

"Your machine is not working!" he barks at me, his nostrils flared. The crowd begins muttering.

My neck stiffens and I grip the controls.

"It's behind you!" Someone in the audience shouts and a ripple of laughter breaks out.

Agrovio crashes around, thundering towards the ball. I fear he's taken too long to react. He curls his foot to hook the ball but misses as it's sucked back by the machine, disappearing off the side of the platform. Gasps fill the studio.

The player leaps off the platform and boots the ball where it hides. Silence follows. Then the control box flashes, *Warning, Warning*. The starter whistle sounds out continuously, and a 'Malfunction' sign appears. Multiple images flood the virtual screen; a goal, a keeper, bulls-eye and defenders all at once. Grandpa grabs my hand from the speed dial and presses the 'off' button.

"Stupid machine!" roars the attacker. "It doesn't work properly." He storms off the stage. The shocked crowd is muttering.

***

190

"That didn't go quite as planned," says Grandpa once we're backstage.

We can't interpret the results because of the control panel malfunctioning.

I slump onto the sofa in the dressing room, arms folded.

"Agrovio didn't like the 'Shunter' much," he says, putting the model train back in his pocket.

"He wasn't very good at it, that's why," I grunt, trying hard not to burp. The baked beans I had at lunchtime are sitting in my tummy, gurgling.

"Perhaps we should've slowed it down when he couldn't keep up," Grandpa points out.

I peel the paper wrapper off my bottle of water and tear it to shreds. It was all going so well until Agrovio broke my invention. Has he ruined my chances too?

49: AGROVIO ANGER

The show goes off air for several hours. We are given dinner but I don't feel like eating much. After a short break, we're transported to Harlimac's football ground with the other contestants.

The coach is hot and stuffy and my eyes keep trying to close. In the seat across the aisle, one of the contestants nods off before we've even driven out of the car park. Must be the effect of the pressure. I nudge Grandpa with my elbow and point at the man. His lips vibrate as he snores so loudly that he nearly wakes himself up. I don't remember him from the clips.

Within minutes of leaving, Reggie's face appears on the screens in front of us. "Hello, you are about to be shown highlights of goals scored, missed and conceded this season. Pay attention as you will need to use this information in your next challenge." I sit up, take a sip of water and stare at the screen.

"A lot more goals conceded than scored," Grandpa groans as he studies the footage.

"Defence is a mess; no one is marking anyone," I mutter. "They need some target practice too." I cover my mouth as I talk to Grandpa in case the snorer is cunningly trying to pick up tips. "Did you see Agrovio miss that tackle and then blame the goal on someone else?"

Grandpa is reviewing Agrovio's profile in the programme we've been given. I look across to see the details. He's the only player to have a full-page spread of his footballing history. Masked by black stubble and greasy hair, Agrovio sneers out of the picture. I shiver as I remember him looming over me.

"These lads need inspiring," says Grandpa. He scratches his chin. "But it's difficult to find anything positive to say."

"Grandpa, I noticed something when I gave the team talk for the final at school."

"Did you?" He scrolls through the players in the programme.

"Yeah, they responded a lot better if I picked each one out individually and gave them a role."

"Ah I see, making them feel crucial to the team."

"Yeah."

Grandpa holds the programme up for us both to study. "Trouble is here, who do you pick out?"

Soon the bus draws into the grounds and Reggie's face reappears on the screens.

"Welcome to the Harlimac Stadium." The snorer sits up, rubs his eyes and squints at the TV. "The players have just done a hard training session. You will be taken into the changing room. Based on what you have just seen, your challenge will be to motivate the players ahead of their televised charity match next week. The players themselves will then be asked confidentially to rank your ability to inspire. Good luck."

"Oh, blimey," grunts the snorer.

The stadium suddenly looks far bigger than when Grandpa and I came on our tour.

***

Seventeen players sit around the changing room. Some are squirting their mouths with water bottles, a few have their heads in their hands, and others lean against the wall, eyes glazed. No one speaks.

All we have to do is motivate them. Professional footballers waiting to hear from me, this is crazy. Blimey, where do I start?

A mixture of mud, grass, sweat and farts invades my nostrils. At least I'm used to it from the boys' changing rooms at school. I think I'm immune to the smell now.

Agrovio spits insults from a corner. "Why've they sent a kid down? How are you going to stop us losing?" Obviously, he hasn't forgiven me for his failure on 'The Shunter'. At least he's sitting farthest away from where we stand.

Side by side, Grandpa and I wait for a moment in silence. I catch my pale-faced reflection in the mirror. I look awful. My palms are sweaty and I'm so thirsty. I'm not sure that I can remember how to speak. In the corner sits Vanson. I feel my cheeks heating up; I'm so embarrassed that I sold him in the one week that he scored. I'm not sure where to look.

It's good to see the friendly face of Maxime Buti, even if he is only a substitute.

"We have a job to do," Grandpa announces, surveying the team.

Snorting, Agrovio gobs on the floor, narrowly missing a cameraman's shoe. Why do fans adore Agrovio? Perhaps he's right, what am I doing here? After all, he is the professional not me.

"You have a crowd of adoring fans waiting for you next week," Grandpa continues. His deep firm broadcast makes me stand taller.

I think about all the kids from school who'd love to be in this changing room. You get one shot at a chance like this and I have to take it.

"Yes," I interrupt. "Paying fans!" My cylinders are firing up. Barney Frank is ready to launch. I'm gonna get this team shunting into action. "And our first job is to change your attitude!"

I try my best to look at no one in particular, having already amazed myself just by talking.

"If any of you have given up, then may I suggest that you leave now." I cannot believe I just said that. A camera zooms towards me. "There's the door," I point behind me. "Do not pass go, do not collect your salary, just leave."

A punchy start: half a dozen open mouths gape back at me, including Grandpa's. The two players that caused Hattie's fantasy league disaster shuffle their boots, their heads down.

What will I do if they all stand up and leave? Best keep talking.

"If you are a loser then you have lost," I spout. "You earn more money every minute, than most of my football-loving friends get in a whole year of pocket money. Even more than Fergus, our goalie, and he does a paper round." I've wanted to say that for a long time - raises a few eyebrows.

The pressure is hissing from my lips. My words are flowing. My arm starts waving at the door, reminding the players of my ultimatum.

"Yet loyal fans still save up to buy a new club shirt with your name on."

I stare at each player in turn, skimming over Agrovio. "Because they want to be part of your club… they are proud to wear your shirt… they want to support you!"

I wait for a few seconds to let my words sink in and give myself time to think of some more. In my head I can see my schoolmates playing in their Harlimac shirts. Barry's is so tight he can barely breathe, and Eddie's hand-me-down is so long he nearly trips over it.

"If you have no supporters, you have no job and no money."

Vanson, my old mid-fielder, is actually nodding.

Grandpa tilts his forehead towards me, urging me to continue. They're still listening. I can't be doing too badly.

"So, before we tell you how to win, I will ask one more time. If you want to give up, please leave now." I hold my arm out towards the door and survey my men.

Agrovio rises, all six feet, two inches of snorting-buffalo anger strutting towards me. "I'm not being told what to do by a kid!"

Grandpa takes a step closer to my side. The giant looms above me. I peek up into his golf-ball sized eyes. He opens his mouth, and I have a full view of all his gold fillings. In my peripheral vision I notice a shadow in the doorway behind Agrovio.

"What are you going to do, little boy? Sack me?" The gold fillings cackle.

Am I?

I remember Dad saying, 'don't stand for any arguing'. I want to make him proud.

I take a deep breath. "Yes!"

I'm not sure I actually mean to say it, but it's what my brain's thinking and it just comes out.

50: MARCHING ON

Lord Loadsa steps out of the shadows and into the room.

I've just sacked his striker! What have I done?

"Agrovio, I need to speak to you in my office," Lord Loadsa says. He doesn't acknowledge me.

"Did you hear what he said?" Agrovio snaps.

"My office please."

Throwing down his water bottle, Agrovio stomps out. The plastic bottle skids across the concrete floor, hitting one of the camera stands.

"Please do carry on," Lord Loadsa says, but he doesn't smile. Then he disappears.

I can't stop now, what's done is done.

"Right," says Grandpa. "We've got five minutes, Barney, let's talk marking."

Time to march on.

"Each of you take a player and watch them like a hawk. You're good at that Ringo," I hold my palm out towards him. "I saw you covering in the Man U match." Ringo sits up and so does Mac next to him. "If there's a player free," I say to the defenders, "don't expect someone else to cover them, call to each other and make sure they are all picked up." Moving on to the attack: "Accuracy is key," I say. "Focus on a point and hit it. Bumble," the surprised player looks up, "I've seen you and Vanson and Zeph working in triangles together, moving your way up the pitch, always being available for your nearest teammate. You can use the short sharp passes to dodge defenders, like Vanson did in the build up to the penalty in the last game of the season." Vanson puffs out his chest. "Most importantly, never give up, that goes for defenders too." I turn round to look at the rest of the team. They're all paying attention.

Grandpa addresses the goalkeeper: "Make the attackers sense your strength. Fill the goal with your stature." He demonstrates, legs slightly bent ready to dive, feet wide apart and arms out reaching for the corners of the posts. "Look that attacker in the eyes," he says, gripping the goalie's shoulders, "and say - 'My goal is to stop your goal'."

The Premiership goalkeeper claps his gloved palms together. He repeats Grandpa's words aloud. He's pumped up.

With Agrovio gone, I'm an attacker down. I walk to where the substitutes sit. "Maxime Buti," I say. He frowns. I hope he doesn't think I'm going to fire him too. "I need you to play up front."

"Moi?" The Frenchman puts a hand to his chest.

"Yes, you have the fire in your belly, remember?"

"Le feu, oui!" He rubs his stomach.

The producer holds up his clapperboard, signalling for me to finish off and for the players to leave the changing room. Players start shuffling to the door. My time in the Premiership dressing room is nearly over. I've done what most kids can only dream about.

I am determined to go out fighting.

"Wait!" I cry. "Come round." I usher them into a huddle. "We are Harlimac FC and we're going to win. Repeat!"

"We are Harlimac FC and we are going to win," they mumble. A bunch of five-year- olds would be a hundred times louder.

"That's pathetic. Louder!" I yell.

"We are Harlimac FC and we are going to win!"

"Again!" I start stamping, and Maxime, next to me, stamps too. It spreads through the players like a wave, until they are all stamping and shouting.

"We are Harlimac FC and we are going to win! We are Harlimac FC and we are going to win!" The noise echoes out of the changing rooms and down the corridor.

"Let's go!" I break up the huddle, shaking the captain's hand as he's first to jog out of the room. The rest of team line up to follow.

Vanson approaches up the line, and my heartbeat soars. Why did I get rid of him? Player after player shakes my hand. Finally, Vanson's goatee is centimetres away from my forehead. I hesitate before offering my hand.

"I'm going to make you proud of me next week, Barney. You'll never want to sell me again," he says.

I hope he keeps his promise.

51: PICK ME

It's nine o'clock in the evening and The Premiership's Football Manager Show is about to announce the live results. We're back in the studio for the elimination round. The audience and viewers at home have been shown clips of our team talks. We don't get to see them, but we can hear the audience's reactions. There's cheering, laughter, jeering and a particularly loud gasp, which is worrying.

Only two contestants can go through to tomorrow's final.

"Take your positions," orders the producer.

Rachel Wise's face is being dusted with a powder puff. A lady from wardrobe is fussing over Reggie's tie. Cheryl with the clipboard is shadowing the producer. One of the contestants makes an emergency exit for the loos.

"Where's he gone?" shouts the producer. "You two, you'll have to shuffle along." He moves Grandpa and me down the line. "He'll have to go on the end when he gets back. We're live in 10, 9, 8, 7, 6," he holds up his hand to signal, "5, 4, 3, 2, 1. Cue music!"

My hands are shaking. If my heart beats any faster I'm likely to self-combust. The deserter returns, dragging himself onto the stage, and stands on the last marker. His face matches the grey of his hair. And I thought my nerves were bad.

Lights in the studio are flashing, spotlights searching through the crowd. I catch sight of Mum, Dad and Hattie in the audience. They sit in the middle of a row, half way back. Leaping out of her seat to catch the limelight, Hattie flings both arms in the air. Dad points at me on the darkened stage then gives a double thumbs up. I clamp my arms to my sides and swallow the urge to wave.

"Good evening and welcome back." Reggie strides out to centre stage. "The elimination round…"

The lights shine brightly in our eyes again. I can no longer pick out any faces in the crowd. Cameras are dancing about the stage, twisting and zooming in and out of the contestants. Beside me, Grandpa tugs at his jacket sleeves and straightens up, standing taller than I ever knew he could.

Our names are announced to the audience. Grandpa stiffens and I freeze. The sound echoes around the studio until the next name wipes it out.

I imagine Al's house with all my teammates watching me on the TV. His dad was making a big shepherd's pie for their supper, and Barry's mum baked a cake decorated as a football pitch. He promised to save me a slice.

"The first contestant to be eliminated…" I hold my breath. Reggie is waiting for his cue. The producer talks into his mouthpiece and Reggie announces the name.

The guy next to us falls to the ground weeping as his spotlight fades. The camera pans away, focusing on the remaining contestants. Two men from the wings walk on to steer him off the stage.

"Keep smiling," Grandpa growls without moving his lips. It's quite a skill to be able to do that.

"We're still in." I try to do the same, but it sounds more like 'worst lin'.

"The next contestant to be eliminated…" My insides feel like I've scoffed a bucket full of ice cream. "Jane Rose…" The army lady! Reggie walks over to give her a hug. The lights spin round to the cheering crowd; they obviously like her. I squint to see if Dad is clapping. She was one of his favourites. It takes a while to quieten the crowd.

More eliminations, the stage is emptying, and still we remain.

Four left.

The final is in sight and I begin to believe.

"The next contestant to be eliminated…" The lights shine on all four spots. Seconds seem like minutes … hours. "George…" Hattie's favourite, the coach of the deaf team is out. Grandpa grips my hand. We're in the final three. I want to jump in the air and wave my arms about. All the hard work was worth it.

Still, I'm sad for George as he walks along the line, shaking our hands. I think he's what you'd call a real gentlemen. Reggie holds the microphone out to him.

"Thank you for your support." George speaks and signs to the crowd. "I've had an amazing time and wish the winner all the best for the future."

A group of boys in a team kit run up to the front of the stage to greet him as he walks off. I wish he was my school coach.

"We're down to the final three," says Reggie.

He brings us closer together, onto the centre three spots. Grandpa and I stand in the middle, flanked by the two non-league coaches. Dad's favourite, Howard Edmunds, is on our left. He's the less experienced of the two, having only coached his team for two seasons but gaining promotion this year. The other man is older; he's been coaching for twenty years in several different clubs.

On the screen behind us they play a musical montage of clips from the show. Grandpa tugs at my sleeve.

"Whatever happens, Barney," he whispers. "I've had the time of my life. Thank you."

I gulp.

"The final contestant leaving us tonight is…" Pulsing music beats around the studio. Reggie waits for the answer. The crowd is shouting all of our names. My head is hot and my hands are cold. A silky thumb tickles my palm. I squeeze it tight.

"Barney and Barnaby Frank."

I feel the weight of the crowd sighing.

"Guys, I'm so sorry. You were great contenders."

Reggie walks over and throws his arms around Grandpa. I'm now swallowing so hard that it hurts. Rachel Wise and Lord Loadsa make their way onto the stage.

"We've put together a special film of just the two of you because you've been fantastic characters to have on the show. In fact, you've been Franktastic!" Reggie laughs, thrusting his microphone under my nose. "Is there anything you want to say to the audience watching here and at home?"

I'm struggling. Rachel Wise is standing next to me now; she bends and kisses me on the cheek. Whistles fly from the crowd. "A kiss from Rachel! It doesn't get much better than that," says Reggie, pulling the microphone away.

"I wouldn't mind one of those," pipes Grandpa. Rachel moves across to him, and Grandpa strips off his jacket to reveal his shimmering shirt. The crowd roars. As she approaches, Grandpa slips his arms around her waist and swings her back like in an old movie. Someone wolf whistles.

"Rachel's been swept off her feet!" whoops Reggie. I catch sight of the front row all in hysterics.

Embarrassing but funny, it gives me time to compose myself.

Get a grip, Barney. All your mates are watching.

Lord Loadsa shakes my hand. "Well done. For someone of your age, you have some impressive ideas." That means a lot to me.

Reggie returns with his microphone as Rachel recovers. "Anything you want to say?"

I cough to clear my throat.

"A big hello to all my teammates watching back home. Don't forget to save me a slice of cake." Everyone laughs. "Thanks to Mum and Dad in the crowd." A spotlight finds them. Mum is hiding behind a handful of tissues, and Dad has an arm around her, screwing up his face. I'm gutted and I expect he is too.

"Thanks also to the Harlimac Harrier."

Hattie jumps on her seat, beating her fists in the air. "I'm sure you're going to be a phenomenal sportswoman in the future. Most of all," I choke out, "to the best Grandpa ever. I couldn't have done it without you."

The audience erupts. Grandpa wraps me in his baboon-like arms.

"Give it up for Barney and Barnaby Frank!" Reggie works the crowd, and the film of our time on the show begins.

My eyes glaze, the screen blurs and a lone tear escapes down my cheek and into the corner of my mouth. I can taste its saltiness.

Apparently, they really liked our ideas but the Premiership's Football Manager Show panel from Harlimac FC eventually said, 'No'.

Our journey is over.

52: PRIDE

"Barney, hurry up or we'll miss the bus!" Dad's knocking on the door.

Tonight it's the charity match for the Premiership's Football Manager Show. Dad's favourite won. I knew he would. He was good.

Should I go to the match or stay at home? I don't want to go and risk everyone laughing at me. School's been weird; no one seems to know quite what to say. Even my friends have been avoiding me.

"Barney." Dad knocks again.

"I'm not coming," I call.

I slip my feet beneath the duvet and grab my pillow. The door handle rattles. Dad bursts in through my barricade of army figures, scattering soldiers across the floor. The door wedges in a pile of clothes.

"What do you mean, you're not coming?" Dad stands in the doorway.

"I don't want to." I twist over and hide my face in the pillow.

"Why not?"

"Everyone will stare at me," my voice is muffled.

"Why will they be staring at you?"

"Because I got kicked off the show!" I shout. "I shouldn't have sacked Agrovio, it was stupid. Anyway, I was never good enough to compete with those other coaches."

I think I'm about to explode. My chest's inflating like a balloon.

Dad sits on the bed and I feel his hand rest on my back.

"Barney, it's OK," he says softly.

"But it's not." I choke on the tears pouring down my face. "It's not OK Dad coz everyone will hate me. Fans love Agrovio, they think he's brilliant."

Dad's hand stays on my back as I sob. I keep crying until my whole body shakes. So many tears it's surprising I don't run out. Eventually, my body sinks into the duvet. Dad slides his arm under my tummy and lifts me up to sit beside him on the bed.

"Why did you sack him?" he asks.

"You see even you think I'm wrong."

"No, no, Barney, I'm not wanting to judge you. I'm just interested."

I sniff a load of runny gunk back up my nose. Nobody's asked me to explain it before, not even Grandpa. I know people are talking about it, and they all have their views, but no one has actually asked me.

"He didn't want to listen. 'I'm not listening to a kid!'" I say in a deep voice. "I know he was 'Player of the Premiership' once but that was years ago. He was the one not scoring goals anymore, and I was trying to help but he wasn't giving me a chance." I wipe my face on my sleeve. "That made me angry. He was so horrible, and I saw Lord Loadsa in the doorway and I knew I had to do something." I puff all the air out of my lungs, my body relaxes and I feel better. I stop shuddering. "I didn't want to be pushed about like you warned me. But I panicked," I admit. "I lost my temper."

Dad pulls me closer. He rarely hugs me these days. It feels good.

"It takes courage to stand in front of all those players and do what you did. It might have been a rash decision to sack Agrovio but I think you inspired the others."

"Do you really think that or are you just saying it to be nice?"

I watch his big brown eyes blinking at me.

"Truly, I think you were Franktastic." He grins, squeezing me tight. "Unfortunately, not everyone in the world is going to be friendly."

I fiddle with the buttons on his jacket.

"People are going to watch the game, Barney. They might recognise you but they're not going to be horrible to you. It's a TV show and they want to see how the winner coaches the team."

Perhaps he's right. They're not interested in me anymore. I'm yesterday's news.

"Grandpa's desperate to go. You know what he's like, he's wearing every bit of Harlimac kit he can find." Dad rolls his eyes. It makes me laugh. He looks at his watch. "There's another bus at quarter past. We can get there in time for the second half. What do you say?"

I shrug. I'm not sure.

Dad jumps up and starts singing. "Goal! Always believe in your boot!"

"How did you know about that?" I bet Hattie told him.

He ignores my question and carries on. "You have the power to shoot." He boots an imaginary ball. "You are incredible!" He changes the words. "Barney Franktastic! My super son." He wiggles his hips. He is a terrible dancer. I can't help but smile. "Come on, Barney, come and watch. Let's see what Howard Edmunds can do for the team."

"He was your favourite."

"No, Barney, you were always my favourite. He was my second, my reserve in case they didn't recognise a class act when they saw one." Dad messes my hair with his big hands. "Come and watch with your proud dad."

I grin. "OK, I'll come, but I'm going in disguise."

In ten minutes I'm dressed in a hat that covers my ears and a scarf that hides my mouth and nose. Luckily it's an overcast and windy evening so I don't look too ridiculous.

53: FACING FANS

Though I can't hear what the crowd is saying, I imagine them sniggering as Grandpa and I walk into the stands. *Can it really be that kid from the show?* One guy definitely screws up his nose as we try to squeeze past him. I march along the row and dive into my seat. However, I find myself alone.

Strolling down the aisle, Grandpa doesn't share my fears, shaking hands with spectators, signing programmes and posing for photos. Even Dad is joining in behind him. The fans like him. But that's because he wasn't the one to sack their striker. I pull my scarf higher up until it tickles my eyelashes.

Grandpa and Dad edge closer until they finally sit down either side of me. After a goalless first forty-five minutes, the second half is about to begin.

"Once in a lifetime, Barney. May as well enjoy it," comments Grandpa.

I peer down to the dugout as the winner, Howard Edmunds, leads his players out of the tunnel. If you stand up straight and tall you appear confident, Grandpa often tells me. Perhaps he gave Howard a pep talk too, because he looks like he's been a Premiership manager for years. Music blasts from the speakers. They even have cheerleaders waving pompoms in the air just like in

American stadiums. Howard claps each player as they sprint onto the pitch.

The opposition's line up is an impressive array of soccer superstars mixed with celebrity players. Surprisingly, we start the second half well with defenders actually marking players – hoorah! The goalie makes a few solid saves but we have no shots on goal ourselves. I can see the black curls of Maxime Buti's hair as he leans forward on the bench. Each time we move into an attacking position, his elbows slide onto his knees, his hands clasped to his lips as if he's praying. Vanson fires a super cross to Agrovio stood on the edge of the box. This is Agrovio's chance to make amends for the cheating penalty he won in the last game of the season. With no one marking him, the striker takes a tap and boots the ball metres over the cross bar.

"You can't hit the target!" chants the crowd.

Another chance lost. Buti combs his fingers back through his hair and holds his head. I've sat on the bench - I know how it feels.

Twelve minutes remaining, and on the half-way line Agrovio loses the ball again. A Liverpool legend sweeps it from beneath his feet. It's hard to get through midfield when you've got someone as good as that holding the fort. Agrovio chases after him and lashes out at his legs. Both players crash to the ground. Blowing the whistle, the ref runs over and issues Agrovio with a yellow card. He jumps up to protest but is pulled away by his teammates – they saw how bad the tackle was.

Without a fuss, the Liverpool player gets up and prepares to take the free kick midway into their attacking half on the left-hand side of the pitch. Harlimac try wasting time. Agrovio crouches in front of the free-kick position and then rolls on the floor, faking cramp. A physio runs onto the pitch, rubs the player's calf and squirts a drink into his mouth.

The opposing fans start booing.

Grandpa nudges me.

Agrovio is getting up and play is about to resume. The only woman on the charity team is waiting right of the centre, dancing about and trying to lose her marker. A high ball pings in her direction. The speedy England player dodges past Mac, collects the ball on her right foot, weaves past another defender and lays the ball off left to a Chelsea midfielder. Slowing the pace, he controls the ball before curling it over to the far corner of the goal. The England lady accelerates with Mac still in pursuit. She jumps into the air and headers the ball past the hands of our diving keeper and into the roof of the net.

"No!" The Harlimac fans around me sink into their seats.

"Bloomin' Agrovio, he can't score and now he's costing us goals too," complains a man in front of me.

The opposition's fans start singing. "We're winning, you're losing coz you can't score. We're winning, you're losing coz you can't score."

The game restarts, with seven minutes to go. It looks as if it'll be another game without scoring for Harlimac. We are no match for these world-class players, even though half of them are retired. The TV winner may be good but he can't work magic.

Howard is standing on the sideline as the game restarts.

Harlimac hold the ball, passing it back and forth in their defending half. Mac chips it into space down the sideline for Agrovio, close to the dugout near where we're sitting.

"Run for it, Agrovio!" shouts a woman in the front row. But he barely moves and the ball is lost off the edge of the pitch. He starts shouting at another player as if it was his fault. An argument begins and they're about to miss the throw in. Howard is on the case: he approaches the linesman, who signals to the ref, and the substitution board is held up.

Agrovio digs his studs into the pitch. He points all his fingers to his chest and stares wide-mouthed at Howard. The crowd are chanting: "Off! Off! Off!" The manager beckons him over and turns to the substitute warming up. The footballer peels off his tracksuit bottoms and jogs up to the edge of the pitch. Bouncing on his toes, he waits for the striker to walk off. As they cross over, he offers his hand out for Agrovio to tap, but the angry striker flings his arms in the air and stomps off down the tunnel, not even staying to watch on the bench.

I want to jump up and shout out to my old friend, but that would reveal my identity.

"Maxime Buti's going on," Dad points out.

"I know," I say, beaming beneath my scarf.

Now I'm the one rocking back and forth on my chair, tearing at my hair.

The throw in is taken and we're defending again, but there's a spark in the team, an energy they didn't have a moment ago. One Harlimac player is creating havoc in the midfield, preventing the opposition from progressing much further. Darting about, blocking possible passes.

The opposition changes tactics and sends a short ball down the wing, but Vanson reads the move and sprints to intersect. Meanwhile, I watch Buti anticipate the break, drawing away from the midfield. This is the team's last opportunity: they can't miss it. I whip off my scarf and stand up.

"Look for Buti," I yell, hoping for an early ball into the box.

"Barney!" booms a voice in the crowd. Al's big brother, the first XI football captain is in the third row, waving at me.

The man in front who complained about Agrovio turns round too. "Hey, you're the kid from the TV show."

Suddenly lots of faces are craning to look at me. I have two options: sit down and hide away or stand up and say what I believe. I stretch my neck and stand on tiptoes.

"Help me chant!" I shout.

"Chant what?" The captain yells back.

"Buti, fire, belly, boot!"

The captain and the surrounding fans begin chanting. The chant is contagious and soon the whole of the west stand are singing, "Buti, fire, belly, boot!"

The ball switches to the far side of the pitch and the opportunity is missed but we are still in possession around the half way line. Our left midfielder is making a slow advance up the pitch. A tackler slides in; our man manages to keep the ball but is quickly surrounded by two of the opposition with no real chance of finding help. The chanting fades.

In desperation our midfielder tries a back kick into the centre, but a quick toe tap from the defender marking him flicks it to the Liverpool legend, who hoofs the ball long diagonally across the pitch. Harlimac's Ringo races towards the ball, clashing with the Manchester winger. We lose the ball to a throw in.

The throw-in is short. A quick cross catches our defence off guard. Vanson barely has time to sprint into the box, only just managing to header the ball away for a corner.

We're outnumbered in the box. Even the opposing centre back, at six foot six the tallest guy on the field, has left his post to try and score another goal. How can our players compete with this giant?

Howard is shouting orders from the sidelines but I doubt anyone can hear him. Don't give up now.

The corner kick glides above the heads of the first few players, the tall guy jumps too early and can't get a head to the ball; instead it bounces off his chest. In the scrum of players dropping back to the ground, the Arsenal striker breaks the defence and the goalie dives short. Then, in a moment of pure genius, Vanson throws his body in the air. He flings his left leg into the goal, catching the ball just as it breaches the line, then boots a long clearance up field. The crowd gasps.

"Astonishing!" Grandpa cheers.

A lone figure breaks early from the mass of players. He tracks the ball in the air. Picking up speed, the player follows the ball's direction. I leap up, rallying my troops in the crowd.

"Buti, fire, belly, boot!"

Dad stands beside me, cups his hands around his mouth and hollers, "Buti, fire, belly, boot!"

Supporters around me join in, the chants surging around the stadium. Grandpa is clapping out the beat.

"Buti, fire, belly, boot! Buti, fire, belly, boot!" Echoing across the ground.

A swarm of defenders sprint after Buti. A mound of dark curls bounce on the head of the lone player as he gathers up the ball and races towards his target. One defender closes in blocking Buti's route to the goal.

"He's skilled him!" cries a lad to my left.

The goalkeeper crouches ready for the attack.

Chanting fills the stadium. Outsprinting the defence, Buti shoots at goal, firing the ball beyond the goalkeeper, into the top right corner of the net. The crowd erupts.

"Goal! Goal!" I cry out in amazement. "We've scored!"

The final whistle blows.

Dancing, Grandpa hula-hoops his hips. Deafening roars fill the ground. Vanson races to celebrate with Buti.

"He scores! Maxime Buti scores!" screams Dad.

The Harlimac fans are jumping up and down, cheering. Buti races back to the dugout and hugs Howard. The whole team is dancing. Harlimac draw, they didn't give up - proof that they can score under pressure.

"Buti!" Dad calls out.

"Maxime!" Grandpa stands on his seat and waves down to the players.

Dad grabs me by the waist and lifts me into the air.

"Buti, it's my son, Barney Frank."

I can see Maxime celebrating with his teammates.

As the player glances up at the fans, Dad bellows. "Buti, my son, Barney Frank." He lifts me even higher; I'm barely balancing.

The school first-team captain in the third row starts shouting my name too, waving at Buti, trying to get his attention. Suddenly Maxime spots me in the crowd and starts waving madly. "Barney!" He points at me. "Barney Frank!"

I raise my hand. My face is burning.

The player holds up all eight digits on his hands. "The fire in my belly!" He cries out loud. He remembers the drill.

The hairs on my arms prickle.

Vanson walks over, swinging his arms across the Frenchman's shoulders. He looks to where Maxime is pointing. Vanson gathers the other lads. Suddenly, the whole team lines up and starts singing:

"B Frank, B Frank, you've got to be frank, be frank!"

People in the rows in front and behind join in; strangers' hands are tapping me on the shoulder and back, ruffling my hair.

"B Frank, B Frank, you've got to be frank, be frank!"

I'm shaking. I'm so very, very happy.

54: THE UNIQUE RIDE

Finally, we are walking out of the ground, alongside fellow fans.

"Barney!" a voice calls out from above.

I know that voice. I look up and immediately spot the red wavy hair bouncing down one of the stadium staircases.

"We scored because of you, Barney." Olive waves before disappearing in the crowd. I feel amazing.

"This is my son, Barney Frank," Dad announces. People start asking for selfies with Grandpa and me. My face aches from smiling and laughing every time I see Dad's head pop up in the background.

"I wish I could travel back in time and relive all the players singing," I say, as we eventually leave the crowds behind, turning down a side street to head for the bus.

"I'll never forget it, son. It's locked in here." Dad taps his head with his forefinger.

"I hope Hattie remembered to record the game on TV," says Grandpa. "I wonder if you can spot us in the crowd?"

"I doubt anyone can miss your outfit Grandpa!"

***

We've been standing at the bus stop for five minutes when a limousine drives along the road and pulls over to where we stand. The blacked-out back window winds down and an elderly hand waves to us. A white-bearded man sits forward.

"It seems we should have listened to you about Agrovio," says a cheerful voice.

"L-Lord Loadsa," I stutter, stepping closer to the car. Dad bends down beside me, peering into the limo.

"Hi, I'm Barney's dad," he thrusts his hand into the car, nearly poking Lord Loadsa in the eye.

"What a fine son you have." He shakes Dad's hand politely.

Dad stands upright, resting his hand on my shoulder. "Yes I know. Chip off the old block." *Really?*

Lord Loadsa addresses me. "Barney, you were right about Agrovio. At the time we thought your actions were rash. Maybe because you were a child we didn't take you seriously enough. I apologise for that."

Lord Loadsa is apologising to me!

"I thought he was right too," pipes Dad.

I don't remember Dad telling me I was right. I sigh. But maybe it doesn't matter any more.

"Well, perhaps I shouldn't have lost my temper. I was very unprofessional," I confess.

"Seems we both learnt a lesson from the show," he says. "Can I offer you a ride?"

Dad is already reaching for the door handle.

"Though I'm afraid I only have two spare seats."

"Oh." I hesitate.

Two spaces but there are three of us. I could go with Grandpa; he is my teammate and he gets on well with Lord Loadsa...

Dad's hand hovers by the door. The Lord is waiting for my answer.

...But I can't leave Dad behind. We always catch the bus to football together, the three of us, Dad, Grandpa and me.

"No thanks," I say, gently pulling Dad's arm away from the handle. His lips open to protest. "We're going to get the bus. It's kind of tradition when we go to a match."

"Right you are. Keep helping your Grandpa with his train set won't you." Lord Loadsa signals to Grandpa, who salutes back. "That 'shunter' technology's definitely got potential." I nod. I'm amazed he remembers everything about us. "It was a pleasure doing business with you, Barney Frank." Lord Loadsa shakes my hand. "I've no doubt we'll meet again sometime."

"Cheerio Sir." Dad nudges in beside me, enthusiastically shaking Loadsa's hand again. "It's an honour to meet you."

I try not to cringe.

Lord Loadsa tips his head. I step back from the car, dragging Dad with me. The dark window slides up. Dad's mouth drops open.

"You just turned down a ride in a limo with a Lord!" He complains, watching the car drive away.

"You can't let celebrity go to your head, Dad." I pat him on the back. "Besides, here's the bus. You ready Grandpa?"

"Yup. You know me Barney, always ready for the ride. Who knows where it might take us."

55: A FINAL WORD

At twelve years old I coached Premiership footballers. Today I am famous but tomorrow I'll be yesterday's news. By the end of the week, I'll be just another kid in the school playground with a lot yet to learn.

Whether you're playing in a team or on your own there are so many 'Franktastic' sports to try. You win some, you lose some, and other sports you do just for fun. Even learning rules and tactics doesn't have to be boring if you're playing a game. I'm good at that bit… sometimes.

Apparently, Dad wants me to learn to play rugby next – oh help! Check out how I get on in 'Franktastic, Tackling Rugby'.

Barney Frank, not average but unique.

THE END.